BE STILL MY HEART

J. L. FEAMAN

Be Still My Heart

By J.L. Feaman

Copyright 2018 by J.L. Feaman

Published by J.L. Feaman

Second Edition

ISBN: 9781728790251

COVER DESIGN—Holly Johnson with HolleHock Designs

INTERIOR FORMATTING—T.E. Black Designs; www.teblackdesigns.com

EDITING & PROOFREADING—MB Saul, Sarah Banks, Gina Casto with Killing It Write

"Lost are we, and are only so far punished,
that without hope we live on in desire."
-Dante Alighieri

PART ONE

W *HAT THE FUCK?*
Leave it to me to be that woman who couldn't get out of her sports bra. These stupid things weren't made for women with curves, yet we're the ones who need them the most. They made no freakin' sense.

I still hadn't mastered shimmying my triple Ds out of one of these things after my morning workout. It was so tight I could hardly breathe and I could never seem to get it off gracefully. I looked like a flailing idiot waving my arms around trying to break free.

I was seriously stuck in this thing and I was going to be late for work. I needed to skip the shower, spray myself with a little perfume, and worry about getting out of this evil device after work.

I hated sports bras, and I hated going to the gym, but at the ripe old age of forty, and newly divorced, it was something new I thought I would try. *Stupid idea.* I was not very coordinated, to begin with, so adding gym equipment into the mix was asking for a trip to the emergency room.

I had always embraced my slightly larger, curvy figure and

working out had never been a priority. My career as a journalist and my family always took priority, but there I was, Amber Johnson, divorced and an empty nester all in the same year and all alone with no more excuses. I guess I needed to work harder to find some.

I got the house in the divorce. It was a beautiful house in the Chicago suburbs, but my ex-husband and his new twenty-something bimbo conveniently moved down the street. He said he liked the neighborhood and just couldn't bear to leave it. *What crap!* He just wanted to rub it in my face that he had a hot new girlfriend. Dave was like that; he was a soul-sucking ass hat. Now, every morning on my way to work as I drove by, I got to see his bimbo dressed in her tight little workout clothes headed to the gym, and today was no different.

"Skank!" I growled to myself as I drove by.

The divorce was probably one of the best things that ever happened to me. We married way too young because he knocked me up my senior year of college. I could have had my choice of men back in the day; I was actually very attractive in my younger years, but one too many shots of tequila and there I was, pregnant with Dave's baby and stuck with him forever.

Don't get me wrong, my son was the best thing that ever happened to me, but my marriage? Well, my marriage was always empty. Every year I spent with Dave I lost a piece of myself. Dave was a selfish man that cared only for himself. I can count on one hand the number of times he told me he loved me in the eighteen years we were together. He never had anything nice to say; in fact, his words were usually cold and harsh. And sex… Well, let's just say my good old trusty vibrator became my best friend. I even named it Ricardo. Ricardo never did me wrong.

I arrived at the office a few minutes late and was greeted

by my tall, skinny, and flawless friend Julie, who appeared very excited to talk with me.

"So, I have this guy I want to set you up with. His name is Matt and--"

"No!" I quickly blurted out.

"Come on, Amber, you have to get back in the game at some point."

"No. No, I don't. I have Ricardo. I'm good."

"Seriously Amber. You need a real man. You can't date your vibrator!"

Julie and I had worked together for almost ten years now. Being my best friend, she has always meant well, but every day it was the same old crap about guys she wanted to set me up with.

"No, thanks. Been there, done that, and we all know how that turned out."

Julie gave me a funny look. She tilted her head and pointed to my chest. "Amber, what's wrong with your boobs? You have a uniboob going on."

"Ugh! It's this stupid sports bra. I couldn't get it off, and I was running late, so I just went with it. It doesn't look that bad!" I proclaimed as I looked down. *Yeah, okay, that's pretty bad, but I really don't care.*

Julie shook her head as she looked me up and down. "Just don't wear that thing on any dates. Speaking of, we need to take you shopping and get you some new lingerie because if your underwear matches that bra, you're in need of some help!"

I heard a distant bellowing coming from my boss, Rebecca. "Amber, are you here yet? I need you in my office."

Rebecca was a mean old twat, but her timing was perfect, and I welcomed her beckoning to get me out of this current conversation with Julie. I grabbed my notebook and coffee, gave Julie a sassy wave goodbye, and headed into Rebecca's office. Julie gave me the usual sad look as if she pitied me.

"What's that smell?" Julie yelled.

I took a quick whiff. Yup, it was me. I guess the perfume shower this morning didn't get the job done. *God, I wished there was alcohol in this cup!* I didn't even really drink, but on a day like this, I could really use a stiff one.

"Amber, sit," Rebecca demanded.

As if I was a dog.

"I have a special assignment I want to put you on. Just hear me out," Rebecca said.

I sat down and rolled my eyes as I settled in for one of her usual long-winded rambles.

"So, do you remember the boy band from back in the 90s? The one that was really popular and all the young girls went crazy for... Oh, what's their name...? I know I have it here somewhere." Rebecca manically rifled through stacks of papers on her desk.

"You mean The Right Stuff?" I questioned.

"Yes, that's them!"

The Right Stuff. Now that was a blast from the past. Back in the day, I was obsessed with them and so was every other preteen girl in the world. I had all their CDs, my room was covered with their posters, and I was infatuated with the lead singer, Kris August, the playboy of the group. They broke up in the late nineties, probably because all their fans grew up and got lives, and their innocent bubblegum-style music was no longer an appeal. A few of the band members tried solo careers, but eventually, they all faded away. All except for Kris. He made a second career for himself acting and had done pretty well. He starred in several movies and was a regular on a popular TV show that filmed in Chicago.

I thought I'd heard in the news that The Right Stuff was doing a comeback tour and every show had sold out in one day. I personally didn't get the appeal. All these grown women in their forties chasing an old boy band like they are twelve years old again. My mind swirled while Rebecca carried on.

"So, what do you think, Amber? Will you do it?" Rebecca's questions snapped me back from my thoughts.

"Yeah, sure," I said even though I had no idea what I'd just agreed to. I was lost in my own thoughts, reminiscing about my past obsession.

"Great. You leave tomorrow." She clapped her hands and grabbed a folder off her desk and handed it to me.

"Wait, what? Where am I going?" *Crap, what did I just get myself into?*

"On tour with The Right Stuff. Amber, I just told you all this. Please pay attention. I want you to write a feature story on the band's comeback and the relationship they still have with their fans after all these years. It's crazy that all their shows are sold out despite not having any new music in over twenty years. You'll be gone for a month, and the magazine will pay all your expenses. I want this story to be perfect; we have the exclusive. Everything you need is in that folder." She paused. "That's all, you may go."

"Um, I'm not sure——"

"That is all, Amber. See you in a month."

Shit.

What did I just get myself into? *That's what I get for daydreaming and not paying attention.* As a writer for *FAME* magazine, I was used to traveling and interviewing musicians, but I've never gone on tour with any of them before.

I can't do this. Can I? Then again, it wasn't like I had anyone waiting for me at home. What did I have to lose?

My wardrobe was pretty basic. It's not like I had a lot of

options to choose from, so why was packing for this trip proving to be so challenging? What did one wear while on tour with a band?

Ugh!

The pile of rejects on the floor ended up bigger than what actually made it into my suitcase. I didn't think anything I owned was acceptable, but since I was scheduled to leave in just twelve hours, my basic jeans, t-shirts, and apparently very unflattering, but practical underwear would have to do. *I should have taken Julie up on the shopping offer.*

I grabbed the remote and turned on the TV for a welcomed distraction. It was so quiet in the house these days that the sound in the background was always nice to have. I attempted to return to the pile of clothes on my bed when I caught a glimpse of Kris August on the screen.

He was walking out of some fancy restaurant with not one, but two extremely gorgeous women, one on each arm, and the paparazzi were swarming in.

Kris had always had a reputation of being a bit of a man whore, but you would think at some point he would have grown up and settled down.

Disgusting.

And this was the company I would have for the next month.

I snatched the remote off the table and turned the television off. *I'm going to be so out of my league.*

I looked at myself in the mirror and dread washed over me. I scooped up the remaining clothes on the bed and threw them into the suitcase.

"I don't even care anymore. I'm done!" I yelled at no one.

I zipped up my suitcase and dropped it on the floor. I was over this day and more than ready for bed, but then I remembered that I was still stuck in this stupid sports bra.

I headed into the bathroom, opened the drawer and rifled through all the crap that had accumulated through the years.

"I know you're in here somewhere… Yes!" I grabbed the pair of scissors and cut each side of the sports bra and tore it off.

"Free at last!" I proclaimed as I tossed the bra into the trash.

I HAD TO WAKE UP AT 2:30 A.M. TO CATCH MY FLIGHT. I WAS not a morning person and 2:30 a.m. was a killer.

I managed to grab a quick shower and a cup of coffee before my Uber arrived, but there wasn't time for hair and makeup. I wrapped my long, dark waves into a bun messily nestled on top of my head and proclaimed myself presentable, or at least good enough.

My flight was as miserable as most flights are. *FAME* booked me a seat in coach and didn't even splurge enough to get me a window or aisle seat. To my left, sat a massive, bulging man with an extreme body odor problem, and to my right, a businessman in his fifties that wouldn't shut up. He kept staring at my chest, too. I eventually put my headphones on. I didn't care if he got the hint or not, I was done.

I arrived in Atlanta, Georgia, at the Park Hotel around 8:00 a.m. The band had been staying here and rehearsing at the local arena for the past few weeks, so this is where we would depart from.

The hotel was huge and had a grand lobby that was fit for a king. It was filled with weary travelers waiting to check out or in search of their morning java to kick-start their day.

I found an open seat in an oversized chair in front of the fireplace and opened the folder Rebecca gave me with all my instructions to see what in the hell I needed to do next.

It simply said: *Text Phil when you arrive.*

I was in the process of texting whomever Phil was when a man dressed in ill-fitting skinny jeans and t-shirt that barely covered his beer belly yelled across the lobby, "Is there an Amber Johnson here?" The whole lobby quieted and turned to look at him.

Oh, that wasn't awkward or anything.

Shocked, I quickly stood up and walked over to him. "I'm Amber."

"Ah, good! Amber, I'm Phil." He held out his hand to greet me, quickly briefed me on the plans for this morning, and gave me the tour schedule to review. "Buses leave at 9:00 a.m. sharp and are parked out back. Jen will be there to meet you," he called over his shoulder as he hurried off to his next task of the morning.

"Great. Thank you." *I guess.* "Who's Jen?" I yelled after him, but he was already too far away and didn't hear my question. I guess I would just figure it out when I got there.

I navigated my way through the lobby to the Starbucks and ordered my usual peppermint mocha. It didn't matter what time of year it was, it was my go-to drink. I stood and waited as the over-energized teens behind the counter rapidly prepared drinks for the crowd of people ahead of me. I knew it would be a few minutes, so I opened the folder that Phil had given me with hopes of learning more about the adventure I was about to embark on. But there wasn't much in there. It appeared to be the schedule, cell numbers of the crew, and some press sheets for each of the band members.

I pulled out the sheet on Kris and found myself entranced by his picture. *Damn! That is one good looking man!* He had the most beautiful naturally tanned skin. I'd always had a thing for men with darker skin. Too bad he's a man whore and totally out of my league.

"Amber, peppermint mocha!" one of the teens yelled.

I grabbed my coffee and headed off in pursuit of a bathroom where I could freshen up, suitcase in tow and coffee in hand while I skimmed the information provided about Kris. About ten steps in I ran right into someone, full speed, sending my coffee flying all over me, my papers, and the poor person I'd run into.

"Oh my God, are you okay?" the man I bathed in my coffee asked.

I looked up to see Kris August, towering at least a foot over me.

His beautiful dark, wavy hair framed his perfectly chiseled face. His tight, plain white t-shirt, now covered in coffee, showed traces of his flawless six-pack that laid hid beneath. He was bigger than I'd imagined, too, with broad shoulders and muscular arms covered in tattoos. Kris August was even better looking in person, and accompanied by a woman I assumed must be his previous night's conquest.

"Let me help you," he demanded as he bent down to help gather my papers that were scattered over the floor, soaked in coffee.

His "companion" could hardly contain her laughter. I gave her the evil eye and then turned back to Kris. "Thank you, but I got it," I barked. "I'm sorry, I should have been paying more attention."

Our eyes momentarily met and I quickly looked away. *Damn, he has amazing eyes.* They were dark and telling like if you looked at them long enough, you could see his soul.

"It's okay, I don't mind." He chuckled. "It's no trouble."

We both reached for one of the pages at the same time, and our hands accidentally touched. I froze. Heat ran through my body like I've never felt before and my heart started to pound uncontrollably. Every ounce of air I had in my lungs fled, leaving me breathless.

What the actual fuck was that?

I hastily collected myself and my papers and frantically searched for the nearest bathroom. "I'm sorry!" I repeated as I ran from whatever the hell that was.

Collect yourself, Amber!

I looked at myself in the bathroom mirror, and saw a mess. My heart still raced, my naturally tan skin was a shade of red I'd never seen before, and my messy bun gave a whole new meaning to the style. And, I was panting like a freaking dog in heat!

What was happening to me? I was always cool, calm, and collected. This wasn't me. I took a few deep breaths to get myself together, and dug out a clean pair of clothes from my suitcase to change into. I combed out my hair, put on some makeup, and took another glance in the mirror, then gave myself a nod of approval before exiting the bathroom.

I completed a quick scan of the lobby to make sure Kris was gone before I emerged from hiding. I didn't see him, so I snuck out and made my way to the buses to meet this Jen girl.

I headed to the back of the hotel as Phil instructed and it looked like a circus. There were eight buses, six semis, and about a hundred people frantically running around. It looked like they'd completely taken over the whole parking lot. How in the world was I supposed to find this Jen chick?

I slowly wandered around, weaving through the chaos, making my way to the buses.

"Are you Amber?" a woman in her late thirties/early forties with hot pink hair asked as she approached me.

"Yup. And I'm guessing you're Jen?" It probably wasn't hard for her to spot me; I'm sure I stuck out like a sore thumb.

"Oh good! Yes, I'm Jen." She smiled. "I'm the tour manager or "mom" as many like to call me. Nice to meet you. I'll also be your roommate while you're on tour with us. Follow me. I'll give you a tour of your new home for the next four weeks."

We walked past a row of large buses which were really

more luxury motorhomes. We arrived at ours, which was black and gray and nestled in between all the madness.

"This is it! Come on aboard. Watch your step."

I dragged my suitcase up the stairs and was in awe at what I saw. "Wow, this is not at all what I expected."

"Nice isn't it? The band really does treat their people right. I was lucky to get this gig." She paused and smiled. "This is the main living area and kitchen. I'm responsible for all the shopping and stocking of all the bus fridges so just let me know if there's anything you want. Next, we have the bathroom." She waved her hands up and down like she was Vanna White revealing a new puzzle on the *Wheel of Fortune*. "Thing is, the water only works when we're hooked up, which isn't often, so no showers."

"Wait, so where do we shower?" I asked.

Jen shrugged her shoulders. "Most arenas have showers in their green rooms, and well, we all just take turns. Also, occasionally when we have days off or we're in one place for multiple nights, we'll get a hotel."

"You're kidding me?"

"Afraid not." She scrunched up her face and frowned.

"And you said most of the arenas; does that mean some don't have showers?"

"Yup! Life on the road can get pretty rough sometimes. But no worries, I keep us stocked with lots of dry shampoo." She turned and continued toward the back of the bus.

Ugh...

"Then, finally, back here are the sleeping bunks. That one down there is yours. Go ahead and unpack and make yourself at home. I need to go check on the guys and make sure they have what they need before we pull out, but I'll be back soon." She gave me a friendly pat on the back as she made her way out of the bunk area and off the bus.

I examined my sleeping quarters. There were six bunks

that looked like little nooks. The only privacy provided were purple curtains that you could close. Each sleeping area came equipped with a small set of drawers, a light, and some plugs. That was it! Imagine a college dorm, but worse.

I did as Jen recommended and unpacked my things. Luckily, I didn't bring much, so it all fit in the small space provided.

I walked out to the main living quarters; a really nice space, modern with black and purple leather seating. Definitely nicer than I expected. The kitchen had stainless steel appliances and what looked like granite countertops. I made myself comfortable on the couch and pulled out my phone.

I fired off a couple texts, one to Julie and another to my son to let them know I had arrived safely.

Julie was quick to respond: *Glad you made it. Now kick back and enjoy and don't come home unless you get laid.*

I responded with a few obscene emojis and chuckled to myself.

My phone vibrated, and I expected to see another text from Julie, but instead, it was from my son. *Love you, Mom! You got this!*

That boy was my life, and he always put a big smile on my face.

"Whatcha' reading there? Message from your boyfriend?"

Startled, I dropped my phone. It was Kris.

How did I not hear him come on the bus?

"No, it was my son. I'm single." *I'm single...really, Amber?!*

"Hey, aren't you the woman from the lobby earlier with the coffee? I don't think we've been properly introduced. I'm Kris August." He held out his hand. "And you are?" Kris looked at me with those dark eyes, waiting my response.

"Hi. Yeah, sorry. That was me, Amber Johnson. I'm the journalist that will be traveling with you for the next month. I'm with *FAME* magazine." I held out my hand to meet his, and he took it with a firm, yet gentle grip. Without skipping a beat, my body reacted to his touch again. Heat raced through my body. My heart was pounding out of my chest, my breathing sped up, and my throat felt like it was closing. I forced myself to swallow, which woke me from my daze. I pulled my hand back quickly.

"Is there something I could help you with?" I asked.

Kris looked perplexed. "I, ummm…was looking for Jen. Have you seen her?" He was staring at me with those dark eyes, rendering me speechless.

I wiped a bead of sweat off my temple. *Say something, Amber!*

"Yeah, uhhh, she just stepped out, but she should be back soon." I pointed toward the door.

An awkward silence stretched out. Here I was alone in a room with Kris August, the man that once filled my teenage fantasies, and…silence.

Why is he staring at me like that? God, I bet I've got something on my face. Fuck! I tried to inconspicuously wipe my face, just in case.

"*Kris!*" someone yelled from outside.

Thank you to whomever that was.

"Oh, I bet that's Jen looking for me. I gotta run. I hope to you see again soon! Welcome to The Right Stuff family," he said as he disappeared down the stairs.

WE TRAVELED ALL DAY AND THROUGH THE NIGHT TO GET TO our first city, which was Boston. We stopped a few times to eat, but I opted to stay on the bus. I wasn't ready to meet the entire band, and I certainly wasn't prepared to see Kris again. Like…ever again.

This was going to be a long four weeks.

Jen alone was a wealth of knowledge. She had been a tour

manager for several bands before this and she spent a lot of time on the road. Too bad I just couldn't interview her and be done.

We talked a lot during our time on the bus, and she filled me in about life on the road while I feverishly took notes. She explained that, for the most part, each morning we would wake up in a new city. The band would do press interviews, sound checks, and meet and greets before each show. Then there was usually an afterparty before the buses would push off around 2:00 a.m.

She told me I had free range to roam and talk to whomever I needed. I just needed to make sure I had my pass on me at all times so security wouldn't stop me. We also worked on a schedule that would allow me to have time with each member of the band over the next few weeks so I could interview them for the story.

I had everything I needed to get started...except for confidence. Dave had really messed me up. I used to be a very outgoing and confident person, but lately, I was filled with self-doubt and would rather be alone. I was really going to have to push myself to get this done because my heart just wasn't in it.

Sleeping on the bus in those tiny bunks was not something I thought I would ever get used to. I tossed and turned all night and found my mind wandering, thinking about how good Kris looked in that coffee-soaked shirt and what other tattoos might have been hidden under it. Dave didn't have any tattoos, and I was intrigued by them. Or maybe it was just the tattoos on Kris I was intrigued by. Regardless, I wanted to know what was under his shirt...and hiding behind those tight jeans.

It was warm on the bus, but I shivered at the thought of how his touch made me feel. Just his hand in mine and my body was on fire. Kris August was not a man I wanted anything to do with, yet I couldn't stop thinking about him.

Sleep finally came to me, but shortly after, I heard Jen get up and leave, so I knew it was time to start the day. I wasn't moving very fast, and I needed coffee badly if I was going to make it through this day. Jen had told me last night that each arena would have dining areas set up backstage, so armed with my "special pass" around my neck, I set off to see what I could find.

As I stepped off the bus, I was shocked to see hundreds of fans lined up, their adoring faces turning my way as they hoped to get a look at their favorite band members. I couldn't help but laugh to myself. *Sorry to disappoint you ladies, it's just me, and I'm a nobody.*

I didn't get it. These women were my age, some even older. Didn't they have jobs, kids, husbands...lives? I couldn't imagine the draw at this age to stand out there all day just hoping to see someone famous. Plus, these guys hadn't even released new music in years. I mean, yeah, they were all nice on the eyes. *But seriously ladies?*

I took out my notebook and made myself a note. I needed to make sure when I interviewed the fans, I found out what the draw was.

I successfully navigated my way through the back halls of the arena and found the food. There were enough tables to seat at least a hundred people and a nice spread had been laid out, but the place was nearly empty; just me and a few of the crew.

I made myself a plate, grabbed some coffee, and chose a table for myself. I opened my laptop and thought it would be a great time to catch up on some emails and document my observations so far, until I remembered the press sheets I still hadn't read.

I fished them out of my bag—they were stained with

coffee, but still legible. Kris's was on top, and his photo taunted me. I quickly turned it over and moved on to read about the rest of the band.

Shawn Daniels was Kris's best friend since grade school and was the second one to join the band. Then there were the brothers, Jason, and Bradley Maddox. Bradley was also friends with Kris and Shawn going back to their school days, and he brought his younger brother Jason into the group.

The sheets didn't share much about them that I didn't already know, but I spent some time doing research online to see what they all had been up to over the past twenty-something years. I found very little on the other three, and of course, tons of information on Kris, every photo op featuring him with random women. Random, scorching hot women. *Typical.*

I must have lost track of time because before I knew it, catering was wheeling in the lunch buffet and the place started to come alive with people. I stayed at my table by myself and observed the new world around me. I knew this was the beginning of the tour, but all these people seemed to already know each other. I guessed they had worked together before while I, on the other hand, felt like the new girl during her first day of school.

Awkward!

I decided to plug in my earbuds and listen to my favorite playlist, simply titled "The 90s". My son was constantly making fun of me for my music choices, or "oldies" as he called them, but something about 90s music made me happy.

I was deep in head-bopping mode, jamming to *"Ice Ice Baby,"* when someone came up behind me and removed my earbuds.

"Whatcha' listening to?" Kris practically yelled as he put my earbud up to his ear to take a listen. "Really? Vanilla Ice. Girl, we need to give your playlist an update."

"What?! I like that song." I snatched my earbud back and turned off my music.

He laughed and sat down next to me with a full plate of food. Shawn joined him.

"I heard all about this mysterious journalist that joined our tour. I'm Shawn," he said holding out his hand. "It's nice to finally meet you."

I shook his hand. "I'm Amber. Nice to meet you too."

Shawn was a good-looking guy; all the band members were. He had short, spiky blond hair and beautiful baby-blue eyes. From what I found in my research, he was recently divorced and workout-obsessed, and it showed. Muscles protruded from his tight Northwestern shirt. *What was with these guys and their tight shirts?*

"Nice shirt, Shawn. My son just started at Northwestern." The thought of my son put a big smile on my face.

"No kidding? My daughter goes there." Shawn had a similarly big smile on his face. You could tell he was a very proud dad.

Shawn was easy to talk to, not at all what I expected. A genuinely nice guy. We spent the next several minutes sharing proud stories about our kids until Kris interrupted.

"Sooo, Amber, are you going to eat? Can I get you a plate?" Kris looked at me with those dark eyes, except, today they looked different. Was it sadness I saw in them or emptiness?

"No, uhhh..." I stumbled over my words. I didn't know what it was about Kris, but he made my stomach feel funny, like I was going to hurl. And that would not be good.

I panicked, and my heart started to race. I needed to leave. *Think, Amber.* I looked at the time on my phone.

"Actually, I have to call the office. I'm late. Sorry to have to leave. Shawn, it was nice to meet you. I'll see you around." I packed up my things and attempted to dial Julie as I stood to make my escape, but I was so flustered that it took me a moment to realize I was trying to make a call from my calculator app.

Brilliant, Amber. Just go with it and keep walking, maybe he won't notice.

I MANAGED TO LAY LOW UNTIL IT WAS TIME FOR SOUND CHECK. I decided it might be good to take some pictures of the band rehearsing, so I flashed security my fancy, laminated pass as I made my way to the arena floor. The band was singing an upbeat song and performing a vigorous dance routine. Impressive for men their age for sure! They were certainly dedicated to their art, and I was mesmerized watching them.

I found myself fixated on the way Kris danced. His body moved effortlessly, sensually, as he grinded his hips. He ran his hands up his body and pulled off his shirt like he was unwrapping himself for me to devour. I felt feverish as if someone had turned up the heat and my body tingled all over.

This was definitely a different show than I remembered from when I was twelve, which was the last time I saw them in concert. This was more like watching strippers perform.

Completely entranced by Kris's tattoo-covered body, I moved in closer to capture this moment on film. I stepped back to position myself to ensure they were all in the frame and pulled the camera up to my eye.

"Shit!" My foot caught on some wires, and I fell flat on my ass.

Fuck, that hurt. Shake it off, Amber!

"Amber! Are you okay?" The music stopped, and Kris was suddenly by my side. He was still shirtless and glistening from sweat.

"Wow!" *Oh my God, did I say that out loud!?* I tore my eyes quickly away from him. Everyone was watching me. "I'm fine...really." I attempted to get up as gracefully as possible without looking at him.

"We really need to stop meeting like this." Kris chuckled as he gave me his hand to help me up.

Completely mortified, I reluctantly took his hand and that all too familiar feeling returned. A sensation of heat and desire flowed through my body. I had never felt this before. *Never!* And I was so confused by it.

He was a man whore, a playboy, not someone I should be giving the time of day to, yet I couldn't stop thinking about what those soft hands would feel like caressing my body, and even now I could feel my nipples harden.

"Ammmbbbberrrrr. You okay?" Kris snapped me back to reality.

"Yes, thank you. Sorry to disrupt your rehearsal." I felt my face flush with embarrassment.

"No worries. Just as long as you're okay."

His smile melted my heart, and his bare chest melted something else.

Keep dreaming, Amber. This man is so bad and way out of your league.

"Really, I'm fine. You should get back to rehearsal. I'm just going to get some ice." I grabbed my wrist—I didn't think it was hurt—I just needed an excuse to get out of there. Kris didn't move, and I could feel him staring at me as I walked away.

THE CONCERT WAS ALREADY IN FULL SWING WHEN I determined it was safe to return. The screams of all those women clamoring for the attention of their favorite band member was deafening. I found a space on the side of the stage where I could easily see the show while keeping clear of the general crowd. Thankfully, there was a barrier up to hold the fans at bay and a line of hulking security guards to keep them in check.

I couldn't believe the level of noise. Between the screaming fans and the music, it was almost unbearable. I had to cover my ears with my hands.

"Here, use these, Ms. Johnson." One of the massive security guards reached into his pocket, pulled out a pair of earplugs, and handed them to me.

"Thank you!" I yelled as loud as I could.

He smiled and nodded. "I'm Donnie. I've been assigned to be your security."

"*What?!*" I seriously couldn't hear him over the noise.

He laughed, got closer to my ear and repeated himself, yelling this time. "I'm Donnie. I've been assigned to be your security."

"I don't need security, but thank you!" I shouted.

"Just doin' my job, Ma'am." Donnie smiled and turned his attention back to the crowd.

Ma'am?! How freakin' old does he think I am?

The fans were so close; just on the other side of the barrier. I would have loved to be able to interview some of them, but I didn't think I would be able to hear what they were saying, so I decided to enjoy the show and take a few pictures instead.

The band was really amazing. I was shocked at the level of showmanship. They were full of energy, charismatic, and you could tell they loved their fans as much as the fans loved them.

Kris was performing one of his solo love songs and driving the fans crazy. He went from one woman to the next in the front row, singing to them and taking hold of each one's hand. Every single one of the lucky women reacted with tears of joy, elated that Kris August had acknowledged her.

He made his way over to the side of the stage I was on and got down on his hands and knees where he seductively and slowly air fucked the ground. The crowd erupted, and I giggled as I watched their reactions. Each one of them was imagining what it would be like to be that ground right now, underneath him.

I returned my attention back to the stage only to see Kris gazing in my direction. I turned around and looked over both my shoulders to see who he was eye fucking, but it was just the security guards and me. My gaze locked with Kris momentarily before I got distracted by a crazed fan trying to get my attention.

"*Heyyyyy!*" She was practically climbing over the barrier, pawing at my arm trying to get my attention. I turned her way and gave her an inquisitive look but said nothing. She looked to be around my age but was dressed like she was a teenager with her boobs out on display.

"*Heyyyy!*" she yelled again. "Are you his girlfriend?" She was slurring her words and was obviously drunk.

"No!" I yelled back, shocked that she would even think that.

"Ohhh!" She paused. "Can you get me backstage?" She struggled to get the words out and spit a little as she yelled "backstage."

Donnie must have noticed the exchange. He walked over, put himself between me and the drunk fan and calmly removed her from the barrier before telling her to go back to her seat.

I turned my attention to the stage hoping to catch more of Kris's panty-dropping dance, but he'd already moved on.

After the concert, I made my way backstage. The crew was busy breaking down the set and packing up the trucks so we could push off to our next city, New York. I was exhausted and decided to skip the afterparty, hoping to take advantage of a free shower while everyone else was either partying or packing up.

The green rooms were marked for each band on the tour and I easily found the one labeled "The Right Stuff." Thankfully, I had taken Jen's advice and brought my shower supplies and a change of clothes with me, so I didn't have to run back to the bus.

I entered the green room, surprised to find it empty, and a little stunned to discover it smelled like a men's locker room.

Although the main room was empty, the bathroom wasn't, so I sat on the couch and patiently waited my turn by scrolling through my Facebook feed to catch up on the world. It felt like a week since I'd been home, but it'd only been two days; this was going to be a long month I reminded myself again.

The bathroom door opened and a huge steam cloud followed the naked man that walked out. No towel, nothing. Butt. Ass. Naked.

"Next!" he shouted as he walked over to a pile of clothes and proceeded to get dressed.

I'm not a prude by any means, but this was going to take some getting used to.

I quickly looked away and claimed the bathroom before I lost my turn.

I turned on the water, undressed and climbed in. The water felt amazing after the day I'd had. I found my mind drifting back to that image of Kris up on stage, wondering what it would be like to be under him as he slowly thrusted and grinded himself deep into my core.

A soft moan escaped my mouth. That man sparked something in me that hadn't been lit in years. It had been a long time since I'd been with a man or even enjoyed sex for that matter, and I wasn't sure I would even remember what to do should the situation arise.

Ugh...Amber!

I was totally disgusted with myself for even thinking of Kris that way. For one, he slept with everything that moved, and two, he would never be into me. Plus, I couldn't even talk to him without feeling like I was going to puke.

I hadn't had a whole lot of experience with men. I didn't date much before Dave, so he was all I'd ever known. And, well, Dave spent most of his time either ignoring me or tearing me down. There was no romance or warm feelings. In fact, up until now, the only one to give me those warm feelings had been Ricardo.

Someone knocked on the door—apparently, I was taking too long—so I turned off the water and grabbed a towel. I slipped on a comfy pair of sweatpants and a t-shirt that hugged my curves, put my wet hair up in a bun, gathered my belongings, and exited the bathroom. I noticed the green room was much busier now as most of the crew had completed their tasks and wanted to clean up before we pushed off.

I decided to head back to the bus and maybe get a little work done before I went to bed. As I traveled down the long hallway to the back door, I saw Kris and Shawn exiting what must have been the afterparty room. You could hear the bass and feel it shaking the walls and floor. And they weren't alone; an entourage of ladies dressed in very little clothing followed.

Must be Kris's picks of the day.

I continued on my way, trying to ignore the scene that was taking place. The ladies were drunk and throwing themselves all over Kris.

"Nice sweats!" he called out as I passed.

I paused and turned around, my gaze focused on several of the women. "I'm going for comfort and practicality, not slutty and whorish." I stared down the drunkards pawing at Kris and grinned. Shawn let out a laugh and held up his hand for a high five. I laughed, high fived Shawn and walked away.

"Iccceee, Iccceeee Babbbbyyyyy," Kris yelled after me and laughed.

———

THE NEXT WEEK PASSED BY IN A BLUR, AND I COMPLETELY LOST track of what city I was in. I buried myself in my work and found ways to avoid awkward interactions with Kris. I kept myself busy by interviewing the fans and was finally able to get time with some of the other band members.

I interviewed Jason Maddox first. He was the youngest in the group and seemed to have it the most together out of all of them. He was happily married with three young children. He shared how hard it was to be away from his family, which is why he was pretty quiet and kept to himself most of the time. I noticed that each night he did his thing, then went straight to the bus. No partying. Jason shared that he was skeptical at first when Kris approached him about getting the band back together. After all these years, he didn't think anyone knew they still existed, but Kris was persistent and, well, he'd pulled it off.

Jason told me he was shocked when he heard the concerts had sold out. He thought it was because they grew up alongside their fans, going through the tough adolescent years together. And now, in adulthood, they could still relate. Fans told him all the time about how this was an escape for them; they were having marital troubles, health issues or whatever it might be, but when they came to the concert, it brought them back to a time when life was simpler.

Bradley Maddox, Jason's older brother, had similar thoughts when I interviewed him. He added that he saw a whole new generation of The Right Stuff fans emerging. The first generation of fans now had kids, and they were bringing their kids to the shows.

It was no secret that Bradley had seen some hard days in the past. After the band broke up, he turned to drugs and hit rock bottom on a reality TV show; like, literally on the show he had a breakdown and checked himself into rehab. But he'd been clean ever since and had become an advocate for fighting depression. He said fans could relate to his struggles and some had said he saved their lives. He got it. Kris had saved his.

When Bradley was at his darkest moments, he told me, Kris was there by his side and even paid for his rehab. So even though he wasn't thrilled about the idea of coming back on tour, and he wasn't comfortable with all the attention, he did it for Kris. Now that he was here, and fans were telling him what an impact he'd had on some of their lives, he was one hundred percent sure this was where he belonged.

I'm starting to see a trend here.

MY INTERVIEWS WERE GOING WELL, AND I WAS STARTING TO enjoy my time on tour. I spent a lot of my downtime hanging out with either Jen or Shawn. To my surprise, Shawn and I had really bonded. We had a lot in common: our kids, recent divorces, and shitty exes. He entrusted me with the real story of what went down: his wife cheating on him with his business partner, for one. After The Right Stuff broke up, Shawn was smart and invested his money in building a gym empire. An empire that was now in ruins thanks to his ex-wife and his ex-business partner.

It was nice to have someone to talk to that got it. He even convinced me to come to the after party tonight. Honestly, I had been avoiding it like the plague, but Shawn promised I would have fun, and Jen told me she would go with me, so I agreed to check it out. Plus, I needed to see what it was all about for the story.

I was just finishing up my makeup when I heard Kris do his usual show closer, "Thank you! We love you," which meant it was almost time. I really didn't want to go, and my stomach was in knots, but before I could back out, Jen came in to grab me.

"Dang girl. You look hot!" she was eyeballing me up and down.

"You think?" I took another look in the mirror. I had on my only pair of skinny jeans, red pumps, and a black V-neck shirt that was revealing a little more than I had hoped, but with triple Ds it's hard not to show cleavage. *Shit, I had cleavage in a turtleneck.*

"Yes! You ready? I need a drink!" She grabbed my arm and pulled me out the door. I could already hear the music, and I saw the line forming at the door to get in. Jen still had my arm and dragged me to the front of the line. We flashed our passes at the security guard, who simply nodded and let us through.

"Jen! It's all girls!" I looked around in amazement. I didn't know why I was shocked. I mean, all their fans were female.

"That's why it's called a pussy party!" Jen laughed and dragged me to the bar.

"Seriously, it's called a pussy party?" I looked at her with a look of disgust.

She yelled across the bar, "Two rum and cokes and two shots of Patron." She returned her attention to me. "And you're surprised?"

She had a point.

The bartender handed Jen the shots.

"Here, take this, and you won't even care."

"Jen, last time I did shots of tequila, I ended up knocked

up." Jen looked at me like I better just drink the damn shot, so I tossed it back.

Damn, that burns. But it feels good.

I choked a few times, and Jen handed me the rum and coke.

The shot took effect quickly; I could feel myself relaxing. In fact, every muscle in my body, my brain included, felt kind of numb.

The party room wasn't as big as I expected; it was just a reception hall with a portable bar, a dance floor, and a few tables and chairs. The music was loud, and the bass vibrated through the entire room. It was dark with the exception of some flashing lights that went along to the beat of the music.

I was in the process of scoping out where to ride out the night when I noticed Shawn and Kris make their entrance. Kris had his usual entourage of women in tow.

Shawn made his way over to us at the bar and gave me a big hug. "You made it! And damn, Girl, you clean up nice!"

I laughed and took a sip of my drink. I noticed that Kris had followed Shawn over and was watching our exchange. I was so uncomfortable that I just kept drinking and before I knew it...yup, drink one was down.

I'm going to regret that.

"Bottoms up!" I slammed the glass on the bar. "Another please!"

Yup. I'm going to regret that too.

The party was actually pretty fun. It felt good to just hang out. Maybe it was the alcohol, but I was feeling pretty good. Jen and Shawn even got me out on the dance floor. I can't remember the last time I'd danced, even though I use to love it.

Kris didn't join us. He kept his distance and occupied himself with his usual hoard of tramps, but every now and then I would catch him staring at us.

"I need a break...annnddddd another drink!" I yelled to Jen as I stumbled my way back to the bar. I asked the bartender for another and patiently awaited his return.

Oh, I love this song! *"Closer"* by Nine Inch Nails came on, and I started swaying to the beat. I thought I was dancing, but maybe I was just drunk and couldn't keep my balance.

"I think you're cut off and you owe me a dance," Kris demanded as he surprised me from behind.

I spun around so fast, I about lost my balance. "Excuse me? I don't think I owe you anything!" But he'd already dragged me out onto the dance floor and, well, I did love this song.

I quickly got lost in the music. I felt Kris behind me, closing in. His hands gently closing over my hips as I sensually moved to the beat. He pulled me to him as his hands slowly explored my body. Heat and desire filled my core, and I ached for more. His lips gently grazed my ear as he let out a soft animalistic growl of hunger.

My body started to tremble, leaving me utterly powerless under his magic spell of lust. I had never experienced anything as erotic as this. It was like we were the only two people in the room.

I could feel his arousal pressed up against me as our bodies moved as one to the music. He pulled me tighter against him as his hands continued to tease me in all the right places. My sex throbbed with desire and begged for his attention. I felt alive, for the first time ever. It was like we were in a time warp; time slowed, and we were out there for eternity.

The music changed, and an upbeat song screamed through the speakers, snapping me back to reality. I opened my eyes and scanned the room to see every female watching our little display on the dance floor. I quickly remembered where I was and who I was with.

What the fuck just happened?

Without a word, I bolted for the door and didn't look back.

And this is why I shouldn't drink.

I stumbled my way back to the bus and settled into my bunk for the remainder of the night. I could still feel where his hands had gently caressed and teased me. It was like my body felt void without them.

What was this man doing to me? I was so confused by what I was feeling, and reminded myself again that I didn't have a lot of experience with men since I'd married so young, and this was all new to me. But one thing I did know was that Kris was not what I wanted. So why did I ache for him?

Was this just a game for him? I'd seen the women he hung around with and I was very different from them. I'm was confused by it all, and it didn't help that the bus was spinning around me. I closed my eyes and hoped sleep would come soon.

"Amber!"

I felt someone shaking me, but my head ached, and I refused to open my eyes. *Maybe they'll just go away.*

"Amber! You alive?"

"Noooooo!" I groaned. "I need sleep."

"Girl, get up! I want to know what happened back there," Jen insisted.

"What time is it?" I slurred as I slowly sat up from my slumber. My head pounded.

"It's 2:30 in the morning. We're just getting on the road again." She sat on my bed and bounced up and down as if that would make me more alert.

"Soooo, dish Girl! What in the hell was that little scene with Kris and where did you run off to? You just disappeared on us, and Kris disappeared right after you. Did you hook up?" She paused. "Because he's bad news. You really should stay away from him."

It took me a minute to get my bearings and remember what she was even talking about. It quickly came rushing back to me, and I felt a sudden urge to throw up.

Wait. Kris disappeared after me? Did we hook up? What was she talking about?

Jen must have seen the look on my face. "Hold on, I have something for that," she called over her shoulder as she took off for the kitchen.

Why is she yelling!?

She handed me an orange Vitamin Water and three Advil. "Here. Take these and chug this. You'll feel better in the morning."

Yes, I was in pain from drinking, but that's not why I was feeling sick. I didn't think some Advil and Vitamin Water would cure me either, but I did as I was told.

"Thank you, Jen."

She continued to look at me, waiting for some answers. There was no way I was getting out of this conversation. "Honestly, I don't know what happened. I had too much to drink, Kris insisted on dancing and, well, I guess you saw what happened, along with everyone else. When I realized what was happening, I left. Alone. I have no idea where Kris went. I'm guessing maybe he was drunk too. It was just a drunken mistake. That's all." I frowned, covered my eyes with my hands, and rubbed my forehead as if that would make it all magically disappear.

"First of all, Kris wasn't drunk. Second of all, it was great to see you let your guard down and have fun, but getting to my main point here, Kris is bad news, Amber. I love him and all, but I'm just being real here and giving you a little advice, woman to woman. You don't want any part of what he has to offer."

Jen pulled my hands off my face. "Look, you see the kind of women he's always with. He's an overgrown playboy. From what I know about him, he hasn't had many relationships, but the last one he did have didn't end well."

I finally looked up at her. "What do you mean it didn't end well?"

Jen let out a long sigh and continued. "I don't know all the details, but before the tour started, we were all briefed on security threats, and there's this woman, Lily, who has apparently been stalking Kris."

"Hold up. Why does one girl stalking Kris make him a bad guy? Famous people get stalked all the time," I defensively questioned.

"True, but the story behind this girl is not a good one. Apparently, Lily and Kris had a thing, and story is he used her, threw her to the side, and moved on to the next one. And, well, Lily snapped. I don't know all the details, but I do know he has a bad reputation with women, so just be careful. I don't want to see you get hurt."

She stared at me with an expression of pity on her face, just like Julie did. I appreciated everyone always looking out for me and all, but I really hated that pitying look people were always giving me as if I was, well…pathetic.

"Thank you, Jen, really. But tonight, was a mistake. I know what Kris is and I have no plans of being his next victim. I'm not interested in him, and he's not interested in me."

I laughed at the thought of Kris August, super star, being into me, Amber Johnson, a forty-year-old sex-starved mother of a boy old enough to be out on his own. "Now, can I go back to sleep? Because I feel like death and need some sleep." I slid down into my bed and pulled the covers over my head.

"Okay, but fair warning, Kris would not have done that if he wasn't into you. I know that look he had, Amber!" Jen warned. "You need to stay away from him."

I waved my hand at her to shoo her away and responded with a mumbled, "Uh huh." *She's still drunk.*

THE NEXT MORNING, I WOKE TO A RELENTLESS, POUNDING headache and I desperately needed some coffee, but first I wanted to do a little research on this Lily girl and Kris to see what I could find.

I wasn't really shocked that I didn't find much; just a few articles about Kris being single and how no special lady had pinned him down yet. I scrolled through images to see if anything jumped out at me, but it was just tons of photos with Kris surrounded by one beautiful woman after another. No news about a relationship, no stories about a relationship gone bad, and no news about a stalker. Nothing.

My head screamed for caffeine so I decided my research would have to wait. I grabbed my magic pass and sunglasses to protect my eyes from all evil light and headed to the arena. The usual groupies were already starting to gather outside, and the crew was busy unloading the trucks to set up for tonight's show.

Waking up in a new city with a new arena to navigate was frustrating. As usual, I found myself lost in search of food services. This arena was particularly huge and confusing, making it difficult to find my way around.

I turned down hallway after hallway and stopped dead in my tracks when I heard someone playing the guitar and singing. This music was very different than the type of music the band sang, but I recognized the song. It was *"(Don't Fear) The Reaper"* by Blue Oyster Cult, but it sounded different, slower...beautiful.

I inched closer to the room where the music was coming from and peeked inside. It was Kris. He sat there alone, looking wrecked like he had been up all night. His hair was a mess, and his face unshaven which added a sexy shadow to his chiseled profile.

He was playing his acoustic guitar while he sang.

He sang it slowly, the melody flowing beautifully from the depths of his soul, but he sounded sad, almost tortured by the words he sang. I stood frozen in the doorway watching him. His back was mostly to me so he couldn't see that I was there.

Every word gripped my heart. Part of me wanted to run to him, and part of me wanted to run away, but I was motionless as I voyeuristically watched, hoping I wouldn't get caught.

This wasn't the Kris August I'd seen while on tour. That man was wild, happy, upbeat, always the life of the party. This one looked so depressed.

Flashbacks from last night flooded through me; the way his hands felt as they teased me, the sound of his animalistic growl in my ear. My body immediately started to respond to the sound of his voice and the memories of his touch. I squeezed my legs together trying to provide the relief my core desired, only to feel emptiness. There was no denying that I craved to be filled by his throbbing manhood.

"Hey, Amber!"

Kris's music came to an immediate halt.

Shit. Fuck!

"Hey, Shawn! I was just uhhh...trying to uhhh...find my way to breakfast. I'm totally lost." *Yeah, lost in more ways than one.* I let out a very awkward and uncomfortable laugh.

"I'm headed that way so I can take you. Are you feeling okay? You look a little out of sorts." Shawn gave me one of those pitying looks.

"Yeah, sure. I drank a little too much last night." I laughed. *If he only knew why I really looked so out of sorts.* "I just need some coffee, and I'll be fine." I smiled.

"Hey, before I forget, we have a day off tomorrow, and a few of us are going to hit the town. Wanna join us?"

"Yeah, I think that sounds fun. It'll be nice to get away for a few hours." I kept my voice low with hopes Kris wouldn't hear me.

We started to walk down the hall when Kris slowly made his way out of hiding. "Who's getting away?" He sounded upbeat and back to his normal self, as if he'd left the somber Kris back in that room.

Shawn and I stopped and turned around. "Hey, Kris," we said in unison. I rubbed my head to get some relief from my pounding headache which now hurt worse. Also, I was shielding myself from Kris, like he wouldn't see me behind my hand. *You're so busted, Amber!*

"Tomorrow for our day off," Shawn proclaimed with excitement. "I've invited Amber to join us."

Fabulous. I should have known Kris would be on this little outing.

"Can't wait!" Kris tilted his head and grinned. "You okay, Amber?"

I dropped my hands and looked up at Kris. He had the smuggest look on his face as if he knew he'd busted me and took pleasure in it. *Shit, did he know I was standing there or is he referring to last night?* Either way, I was so done with this situation.

"I'm *fine*! Can we please just go get some freakin' coffee!" I turned around and started walking as if I knew where I was going, but after just a couple of steps, I stopped. "Can someone *please* show me where the freakin' coffee is?!"

Kris laughed. He was definitely enjoying my discomfort.

Asshole.

I waited until they both caught up with me and let them lead the way.

I DRAGGED THE ENTIRE DAY, AND I COULDN'T WAIT TO GET TO bed. I was actually excited about the day off tomorrow.

As soon as I finished up with my post-show fan interviews, I grabbed my bag and headed for the showers. My last task of the day before I could collapse in my bunk!

The green room was quiet, just as it usually was this time of night. Most of the crew were either packing up or already at the party. There was someone already in the shower so I had to wait my turn. As I always did in this situation, I made myself comfortable on the couch and struggled to stay awake. In fact, I thought I may have dozed off as I was startled by the sound of the bathroom door opening.

"Sorry, I didn't mean to wake you," Kris said. He stood there in nothing but a towel, his body glistening with lucky little beads of water from the shower.

I was confused, not only because I had just woken up, but my brain couldn't handle what I was seeing. This man's body was flawless and covered in the most beautiful display of tattoo art I had ever seen.

"Why aren't you at the party?" I questioned as I tried not to stare at the perfectly formed V on his lower abdomen which had my mind begging to see what pot of gold was at the end of that rainbow.

"I don't know, I just didn't feel like it tonight," Kris somberly said as he slowly towel-dried his hair. He stopped and looked at me with that mischievous grin of his.

"Is there something more I can show you?"

Shit!

It must have been obvious that I was staring at him. I quickly jumped up and grabbed my things. "You're so arrogant, Kris. Is the shower free or are some of your groupies still finishing up?" I barked at him. Maybe a little too harshly, but still...

"It's all yours," he said as he nonchalantly dropped his towel and grabbed his jeans.

I gasped. I didn't mean to, but he was fully aroused, and oh my God, he was huge. I tried to cover up my gasp with a cough as I swiftly turned away and shut the bathroom door behind me.

Smooth, Amber!

I stood against the bathroom door, frozen. If I moved, I would probably collapse. I needed a second to catch my breath.

"It's all yours." Those words kept repeating in my head. I wondered if he meant the bathroom or that amazing erection. That man drove me crazy in more ways than one. I knew what Jen said, but would it really hurt to just fuck once and get it out of the way? People did it all the time, right?

I couldn't get the image of his hard cock out of my head. Giving oral sex was never my favorite because well, my ex was an asshole, but I wanted nothing more than to lick Kris's hard, throbbing erection and taste his manhood.

"Ummm, Amber?" Kris knocked on the door.

"Yeah?" I sheepishly replied.

"You dropped your shampoo."

I looked down at my supplies, and sure enough, my shampoo was gone. I must have dropped it as I stood there hypnotized by his magic wand.

I slowly cracked the door open and stuck out my hand as I didn't trust myself to see him again. He turned my brain into mush, and my vagina took over and did all the thinking. I mean, I didn't even really know this guy, yet all I could think about was having him impale me with his monster cock.

He gently placed the bottle in my hand, and I quickly retreated back into the safety of the bathroom and shut the door.

I made my way into the shower and let the water run over

me as I pulled myself together. Then I started to cry. Why? I didn't know. Maybe because I was overwhelmed. Maybe it was confusion again. I was lost. And, I was sexually frustrated. Everything just hit me like a ton of bricks.

What was this man doing to me? I had never felt this intense desire toward anyone before. I had never craved the feeling of someone's hands on me like I craved his.

I couldn't just ignore these feelings, could I?

Was I feeling this way because I was star-struck? I didn't think so. I had been around plenty of celebrities and never had these kinds of reactions.

What Jen told me about him had been echoing in my head. But I searched, and I found nothing about Kris and Lily online. Which didn't mean it didn't happen, but it's pretty hard to hide those things when you're famous. And of all the people I'd talked to, the band, the fans, they all idolized Kris. I had documented tons of stories about how he had gone above and beyond for people time and time again.

He had a kind heart somewhere behind that playboy exterior.

I couldn't lie to myself; this man scared the shit out me. The way he made me feel? Scary! The fact that I felt so strongly even though I didn't even really know him yet? Stupid scary. His bad reputation as a playboy and the fact that I was pretty sure he was just playing with me, and, there was no way he would even entertain the idea of having sex with a woman like me...? Yeah, that's outright terrifying.

I lost myself eighteen years ago when I married Dave. I gave up who I was in an attempt to be a good wife to a man that didn't even like me. I sacrificed my own happiness for the well-being of my son, and I didn't regret that. Dave may have been a horrible husband, but he was a great father.

So here I was, forty years old, empty, afraid, and lost. I had no idea how to love or be loved, I had no idea how to date, I had no idea how to even enjoy sex, and it was time I changed that.

I felt ashamed because of these sexual feelings I had toward Kris, but why? I'm a grown ass woman. *Why can't I have a little fun? What's stopping me?*

Am I afraid of what people will think? Fuck them. Am I afraid of getting hurt? Yes, but I'll never find happiness if I don't go after what I want.

Everything I'd ever wanted was on the other side of my fears, and it was time I faced them head-on. I've hidden behind my pain and insecurities for far too long.

I wiped away my tears and held my head up high. Tomorrow was a new day, and I was going to be a new Amber. I'd already seen small glimpses of myself begin to emerge during this trip, but it was time I fully awakened from my eighteen-year slumber. And whether it was Kris or someone else, it was time to let down my guard.

PART TWO

I T WAS A BEAUTIFULLY WARM morning; the sun was shining, and it felt amazing on my skin. I wanted to take in as much sun as I could so I slowly made my way over to the waiting SUV that was going to take us to some top-secret location for some fun time during a rare day off. I could not believe how hard these guys worked. They went weeks without a day to catch their breath.

I felt surprisingly good after my little meltdown last night. I took a little extra time to curl my hair and perfect my makeup, hoping to add a little confidence to go with my new attitude. It's not that I had never done those things before; they just weren't usually things I felt like I needed to spend a lot of time on. I was who I was, love it or leave it!

I arrived to find Kris and Shawn leaning up against a very nice, black, Secret Service-looking SUV. They looked like models at a car show. They were both dressed in jeans and tight-fitting t-shirts. Both looked amazingly hot. *Damn!* I giggled and shook my head as I made my approach.

"It's about time," Kris smirked at me.

I looked at my phone to check the time, I knew I wasn't

late. "You said 10:00 a.m., It's 9:59; I'm on time," I proudly proclaimed as I mic-dropped my phone back in my purse.

He reached inside the truck and pulled out a very large cup of Starbucks coffee, "Here, I got you this." He looked like a shy young boy handing a girl a Valentine's Day card for the first time.

"Thank you, Kris. That was…nice." I was totally taken by surprise. Definitely not something I had expected from him.

"Well, yesterday you were a little…well…bitchy until you got some coffee, so I wanted to make sure you didn't ruin our fun today," Kris matter-of-factly stated as he handed me the cup of coffee with that boyish grin of his.

Smug bastard! If he only knew the real reason why I was so "bitchy."

I took a sip of my coffee as I tried to think of a way to respond to that comment. "Mmm! Is this peppermint mocha? God, I've been craving one of these. This is my favorite; how did you know?" I excitedly questioned.

"Well, you did kinda spill yours on me, and I smelled like peppermint candy all day, so it was kinda hard to forget." He stared at me with his amazing eyes, and I quickly forgot about the bitchy comment and remembered what an ass I was, spilling my coffee on him that day at the hotel.

"Yeah, sorry about that again. I guess I'm all about great first impressions." I laughed uncomfortably. There was an awkward silence. "So, where's everyone else?" I looked around, and it was just the three of us still.

"Just us today. Jason's family is in town, and Brad's hanging with them. I think the crew's all catching up on some sleep and Jen is running errands."

"And where's your entourage of ladies, Kris?" I smugly questioned.

"That's why you're here, Amber," Kris sarcastically answered.

But the way he was looking at me gave a very different vibe. He was staring at me like I was going to be his breakfast. He even licked his lips like he was about to come in for the kill.

Shawn opened the door and motioned for me to get in, and I happily obeyed.

"Hello, Ms. Johnson," Donnie welcomed me from the driver's seat.

"Hey, Donnie." It was nice to see another familiar face joining us.

Kris slid in next to me, and Shawn piled in next to Kris closing the door behind him.

I couldn't help but notice how close Kris was to me. That all too familiar heat began to overcome me. God, and he smelled amazing. I didn't know what he wore, but it gave me butterflies in my stomach. I cracked the window as if some fresh air would cool me down, knowing damn well nothing could cool off my desires, but it was worth a try.

"Hot flash?" Kris laughed.

"Ha, funny." I couldn't be any more sarcastic if I tried.

I scooted as far away from him as I could get; I was practically plastered to the door. "Um, so where are we going?" I looked at Kris and then at Shawn, but they both just smiled and said nothing.

"You guys aren't like secret killers or anything are you? I mean, I don't really know you all that well... I'm kind of second guessing my decision to get in a car with you. I'm so much smarter than that!" I paused, still nothing. "All righty then, you're totally taking me to a forest to kill me. Good job, Amber!" I said to myself as Shawn and Kris just looked at each other and started laughing.

"Seriously, Amber, you're killing me," Kris said. "I have everything under control. Just sit back and enjoy."

I looked at Shawn for answers.

"Don't look at me. He hasn't even told me where we're going." Shawn smirked.

"Fine, but if I end up dead, I'm coming back to haunt you both!" I joked.

I sipped on my coffee and smiled at how thoughtful Kris was. I mean really, he remembered what type of coffee I spilled on him.

"So, Amber, I heard my big day with you is tomorrow?" Kris turned and glared at me.

Big day? As in gonna let me take a ride on the Loch Ness monster?

"What big day might that be?" I seriously couldn't think of what he might be talking about. My vagina, on the other hand, was hoping it was going to be her lucky day. I gracefully crossed my legs and uncomfortably shifted to shut her up.

"Our interview?" Kris reminded me. "I'm looking forward to it."

"Oh, yeah. Sorry. I seriously don't even know what day it is. It's hard to keep track these days. I don't know how you guys do it day in and day out." I let out another nervous laugh. "I honestly don't even know what state we're in."

Kris laughed. "It's Wednesday, we're in Texas, and arriving at our first destination."

I sighed with relief that the car ride was short. I looked out the window as the SUV slowed and pulled into what appeared to be a huge amusement complex. The parking lot was empty. "It looks closed?"

"That's because it technically is." Kris smirked.

"I'm not breaking in!" I quickly snapped.

"We are not breaking in," he replied. "I rented it out for the day." Kris reached over me, opened the door and practically pushed me out. He was like a kid on Christmas morning; he seemed so excited.

I stood there and waited for Shawn to get out. "Are we doing this?" I jokingly asked.

"We're doing this," he responded as we followed Kris, who was already at the entrance impatiently waiting for us.

The place was huge! It had an indoor roller rink, bowling, laser tag, go-karts, and an arcade. I had been to places like this before with my son, and thought I actually might enjoy this.

Kris reappeared. He was jumping because he could hardly contain his excitement.

He's such a big kid.

"Here. Use this card. It's fully loaded so you can play whatever you want," Kris handed Shawn and I both a game card. "Also, I opened a tab for us. The bartender will be by soon with our first round."

"Kris, it's still morning. I haven't even finished my coffee yet." I held up my coffee to make a point.

"Chug it down, girl. I ordered you a beer." Kris smiled devilishly as he took off to his first game.

We played games for a few hours. Kris and Shawn dominated me in every single one. We shot baskets, and I missed every shot. I even took a ball to the head—my own ball. Yeah, that takes skills right there.

We had a Pac-Man tournament where I came in a close second place. We even played Skee-Ball which I loved but I'm obviously out of practice at it because three of my balls ended up bouncing back at me. Kris and Shawn were practically in tears laughing at my failures. I couldn't help but laugh at myself too. I was having a really good time, but I'm super competitive, and I was bound and determined to find something I could win.

Racing!

"I think it's time for some go-karts!" I yelled as I ran off in that direction. I swiped my card and climbed in a shiny red car with my lucky number, thirteen, on it. Kris and Shawn followed and jumped in cars behind me.

"You're going down!" Shawn yelled.

"Bet! Game on!" I returned my focus back to the track, and the moment the light turned green, I hit the gas at full speed. If there was anything in this place I was good at, it was driving. I always secretly thought I should have been a race car driver.

I loved the wind in my hair and the feeling of gliding around the corners.

Kris was on my tail, but I kept to the inside and made sure he couldn't pass me. Shawn on the other hand must have had a super slow car and fell way behind. I caught a glimpse of him as I rounded a corner and saw he was cursing out his car, and I couldn't contain my laughter.

With every lap, he fell farther behind, and I made sure to wave as I lapped him. He had a few choice words for me and gave me the finger.

The light flashed yellow which meant the last lap, and I was still in the lead. *I got this!* Kris was still close behind me. In fact, I was pretty sure he thought this was bumper cars because he was getting so desperate that he was now trying to get me to spin out by bumping the back end of my hot little red car.

Not gonna happen, buddy!

I unexpectedly swerved out of the way as he came in for another bump causing him to miss and spin out as we rounded the last corner.

I crossed the finish line. First place!

Victory was mine! Finally!

I got out of the car and did a very classy celebratory dance as Kris and Shawn finally pulled in behind me. Both were swearing and making up excuses as to why they lost. I, on the other hand, couldn't stop laughing. I danced my way over to them. "In your face!" I cheered.

"Man, I'm done with that shit! That was bogus! I'm gettin' a drink." Shawn walked away toward the bar, defeated.

Kris had that devilish smirk on his face as he walked toward me. I slowly backed up until I was against a wall and couldn't move any farther. He came in so close I thought my heart stopped. I gasped as he gently placed his hands on my hips.

"Okay, Miss Sassy Pants, that was hot, but I want a rematch."

I could feel his bulging monster gently brushing up against my mound. I subtly squirmed with hopes the friction would give some relief to my throbbing groin. Our eyes were locked, and I was frozen.

Did he seriously walk around 24-7 with a hard-on? Snap out of it, Amber!

I knew what he was doing. He was trying to get me all worked up to throw me off my game. Typical man, thinking he could use his good looks, sexy smelling body, and very... large...hard...cock to distract me.

I squirmed again.

Well, it was not working... Okay, maybe it was working a little. I was totally weak at the knees and not even sure I could walk.

I smiled, leaned in close and whispered in his ear, "Game on!" I pulled away from his magic grip and walked back to my hot little red car.

"Game on!" Kris said as he passed me to get to his car. "And loser gets a tattoo, winner's choice."

"What!? Hell no!" *He's fucking crazy.* "You're fucking crazy!" I was not agreeing to that. Easy for him because he was already covered in them; but I had a fear of needles, and as much as I loved tattoos, I could never get one.

"Then you better win!" Kris laughed as the light turned green and we took off.

Shit!

As we approached the first corner, I was barely holding it together. I was frantic thinking about having to get a tattoo, my legs were still weak from Mr. Big Dick, and the vibration of the go-kart was teasing my already sensitive and very neglected lady bits. I was so lost in my own thoughts that I didn't even notice Kris sneak up beside me and take the lead.

Kris waved at me and smiled as he pulled out in front of me.

"Fuck you!" I screamed as I rammed into the back of him.

Okay, maybe that was a little extreme, Amber, but you cannot lose!

Kris was laughing at my obvious distress.

Whatever I did, I couldn't pass him. I was swerving all over just trying to catch him off guard, but nothing worked.

Yellow light. Last lap.

Shit, shit, shit! Pull it together, Amber!

My efforts all failed. My last-ditch attempt to take the lead made me spin out just like he did during the first race. And just like that, I lost!

I watched Kris cheerfully cross the finish line, mocking my previous victory dance. I slowly pulled my car in and got out. Kris was anxiously awaiting my arrival.

"You're getting a tattoo! And I get to pick it out," Kris proudly proclaimed.

I just kept walking; hoping if I ignored him, he would go away. No luck.

Shawn appeared with a round of beers for everyone. I grabbed mine and kept walking.

"What's gotten into her?" Shawn asked Kris.

"She's mad because I beat her and now she has to get a tattoo." Kris laughed.

"Damn! That's awesome! Amber, don't be mad. It'll be fun… We can all get one," Shawn said trying to comfort me.

I stopped. Took a long sip of my beer and responded. "Fine. But can I at least get some lunch first? I'm starving." I crossed my arms and waited for them to catch up.

I admit I'm a very sore loser, but despite my fear, I had always secretly wanted a tattoo, so it appeared this was going to happen. Even if Kris did play dirty to win. I think I was angrier at the way he toyed with me than I was at the fact that I'd lost.

We grabbed a table at one of the bowling alley lanes. Kris wanted to bowl a game while we waited for our lunch.

"Amber, grab a ball," Kris demanded.

"No, I'm good," I responded without even looking up at him. I was at the table scrolling through my Facebook posts.

"You're not going to bowl?" Shawn asked with those damn puppy dog eyes.

"Shawn, I really hate bowling. It's just not my thing."

"*Please*," he begged.

"Ugh. Fine. I'm just warning you, I really suck at bowling, and after the day I've had with balls, this is not going to end well." I stormed off to find a ball and Kris and Shawn erupted in laughter. "I didn't mean it that way, you toddlers!" I yelled back.

I returned with a puke green, nine-pound ball and placed it in the holder, then went back to the table to reclaim my seat where I was hoping to ride out this game. Kris was messing with the screen, trying to come up with fun names for everyone and Shawn joined me at the table.

"You know, he's not a bad guy." Shawn looked at me with a concerned expression.

I was a little taken aback by his comment. "I…I never said that he was. Where is this coming from?"

"I don't want to get involved, but I just wanted to put that out there. Just get to know him a little. You'll see." Shawn smiled as he got up to walk away and took a seat at the score monitor.

"Wait! Shawn!" I yelled after him. "There's nothing to get involved in!" What was he talking about?

"What's all the yelling about?" Kris interjected. "You're up first, Amber."

Shit!

I really wanted to find out what Shawn was talking about. I grabbed my puke green ball, walked up to the line, and chucked it down the lane. It rolled immediately into the gutter.

I don't even care.

Kris and Shawn clapped. I turned around and gave them both the death stare. I impatiently waited for my ball to be returned, picked it up, walked back to the line, chucked it again, and into the gutter it went.

I marched my way to the open seat next to Shawn, eager to finish my conversation with him. Thankfully, Kris was next, and he was already up, waiting to show us his bowling skills.

"Nice job, Sassy Pants," Kris teased as he walked by.

"Sassy Pants?" I questioned.

Kris pointed up to the screen, "Yup! That's your new name." He turned around and headed down the lane to make his first throw.

I rolled my eyes and gave him my best sassy smile before I quickly sat down next to Shawn. "What did you mean when you said you don't want to get involved. Get involved in what exactly?" I whispered to make sure Kris couldn't hear me.

Kris threw his ball. It just barely escaped the gutter, then clipped one pin, knocking it down. "It's all good. I'm just warming up," he proclaimed.

Shawn laughed. "You suck, August!"

"Shawn!" I playfully pushed him trying to regain his attention.

"Look, I just think you might see Kris in a different light than who he truly is. He's a good guy, and there's more to him than what you see," Shawn explained. "I think you two might benefit from getting to know each other a little better. That's all," Shawn finished with a wink as he stood up to take his turn.

Ugh... That told me nothing!

Kris returned and took Shawn's seat next to me. "So apparently I suck at bowling too. It's harder than it looks." He looked at me, defeated.

"Wait, you've never bowled before?"

"Nope. This is a first."

"Wow, something Kris August isn't good at! I might need some pictures of this for the article," I joked.

"I'm an open book, Amber. Write whatever you want." Kris placed his hand on my knee and gave a little playful squeeze. "I have nothing to hide. Not even my horrible bowling skills." He smirked as he playfully and slowly slid his hand up my thigh. Not getting too close, just testing the waters. "But I have many other things I'm good at that I would be happy to show you."

I jumped up. "Yup! I'm sure you do!"

I hated the way my body reacted to his touch. It was like I lost all control of myself when he touched me. I mean, yes, it'd been a long time since I had been with a man, but I felt like a hormone-raging teenager when he touched me.

Don't get me wrong, his touch felt amazing, and it seemed to be all I could think about these days, but at the same time, it was terrifying how much control his touch had over my body.

"It's my turn again!" I yelled as I rushed away to grab my ball.

Pull it together, Amber!

His one little touch had my body trembling with desire. I had a hard time holding the stupid ball. I swung my arm back to get some momentum and flung the ball forward so hard and with so much momentum that it went directly into the lane next to ours, and of course, right into the gutter.

"Now that takes some skill." Kris clapped. "Damn, girl! I know I haven't played before, but I'm pretty sure you're supposed to throw the ball in this lane," he said as he buckled over with laughter.

I couldn't help myself; that was pretty funny. I joined both Kris and Shawn in their laughter. I gracefully bowed at my performance. "I think I'm done. Kris, you can finish my turn!"

Kris happily jumped up. "Well, I can't be any worse than that!"

I was just getting ready to finish questioning Shawn about his odd comment when the food arrived. Shawn jumped up. "Yes! I'm starving. Kris, food," he yelled as he ran to the table.

Looked like this conversation would have to wait.

Next thing I knew, Shawn conveniently excused himself so he could take a phone call, leaving just Kris and me to eat...alone.

This won't be awkward... Ha!

"Pass me the ketchup," Kris demanded.

Even though the table wasn't that big and I could probably hand Kris the ketchup, I decided to throw it at him. "Catch!" I yelled as I tossed it toward him.

Kris caught it and proceeded to smother his French fries. "So, Amber, what's your story?"

"My story?"

"Yeah, your story. Everyone has one."

"Hmm, good question." I sat there for a minute to think about how to respond and was at a loss. *What is my story?* "I'm the journalist; isn't it my job to learn about your story?" I teased.

"You'll get your chance with me tomorrow so it's only fair I get to learn a little about this mystery woman named Amber," Kris smiled.

"Okay," I laughed. "I guess that's fair. Well, I grew up in the Chicago suburbs, where I still live now. Went to college to study journalism, but I guess you already knew that. I got pregnant and married way too young, in that order." I paused and took a sip of my beer before continuing. "My marriage was horrible, but I got an amazing son out of the deal. He just went away to college this year, and I miss him horribly. He is truly the only good thing in my life.

"I'm recently divorced, but my ass hat ex moved down the street with his twenty-something new piece of ass, so that's great." I paused and took a longer chug of my beer. "I love my job. I get to travel and meet great people. So, there's that."

I looked up at Kris who was very attentively looking at me. "I love music. I actually used to write some when I was younger, but I haven't done that in years. Which is why I guess I love my job. I get to hang out with some pretty brilliant musicians and tell their stories."

I let out a little uncomfortable giggle. "I don't know, I'm just a simple woman I guess. Not much more to tell."

"This ex of yours, did he hurt you?" Kris angrily questioned.

"God, no. No. It wasn't like that. We just were never right for each other. We only got married because I was pregnant. We had nothing in common. We tried for a while to make it work, and then I think we both just gave up. Well, he gave up. I always tried to be a good wife, and I just didn't get anything in return. I gave and gave and, well, he took and took. Shit, I think I can count on one hand how many times he ever told me he loved me. We didn't fight or anything like that. We just didn't talk, and when we did talk, he was usually criticizing me; I couldn't do anything right. I think he resented me for getting pregnant." I looked down and took a big deep breath.

"He sounds like a fucking coward to me. Why did you stay with him for so long? I mean don't you feel like you maybe missed out on something?"

"I stayed for my son." I took another long drink of my beer. As if the beer was going to make it easier to talk about this with Kris. Actually, it was helping. I hadn't felt this comfortable talking to anyone in a very long time. "Dave was a good father, and I felt like my son deserved a normal family. Well, as normal as a loveless marriage could be. We were able to give him a good childhood and happy memories. It was a sacrifice I chose to make for him. Plus, I'm very independent and never really felt like I needed Dave, so I didn't care that he was absent from my life. I'm pretty sure he was cheating on me for most of our marriage, but I honestly didn't care. It's not like I wanted him." I laughed.

"I guess I didn't know any different. I can't say I've ever been in a loving relationship; that was all I've ever known so I didn't have anything to compare it to and I honestly don't know if I feel like I missed out on anything. I mean, yeah, sure, I wish things would have been different." I paused.

"I know that might make me sound weak or like a doormat, but it wasn't like that. I just put my son's happiness before mine. That's what you do as a parent."

"I can tell you really love your son. I can see it in your eyes when you talk about him. I bet you're a great mother." He paused. "I've always wanted kids, but it just never happened for me." He smiled, but I could see the sadness in his eyes.

Kris wanted kids! Holy crap, that was not something I expected.

"Hey, you wanna finish our game?" He was obviously trying to change the subject.

"No. I think I've had enough bowling for today." I snickered.

"Yeah, me too." He laughed. "I think it's time we found Shawn and got out of here. You have a tattoo to get."

"You're seriously holding me to that?"

"Yes, but I promise I have something perfect in mind for you." Kris excitedly jumped up, "Let's roll!" He put his hand out like a gentleman to help me up, and I hesitantly accepted.

We climbed back into the SUV, and I closed the door behind me.

"Donnie, take us to James's, please," Kris instructed.

"James's?" I questioned.

"Yup. He's a buddy of mine who lives down here. He owns a tattoo shop conveniently around the corner," Kris smirked.

"Is there anything I can do to get out of this?" I frantically asked.

"Hmm, well maybe…" He winked at me.

"Nope. Tattoo it is," I conceded.

We quickly arrived at James's; it was literally around the corner from where we were. It was a small tattoo place and looked like a dive from the outside, but the inside was nice and looked clean. *Not like I had anything to compare it to.*

"Kris, my boy! Long time!" A bald, heavily tattooed man met Kris at the door with a manly, bromance hug.

"James! Long time, brother! Thank you so much for fitting us in on such short notice. You remember Shawn, right?"

"Yes. Shawn, how's it going?" James asked.

"Hey, James. Good to see you," Shawn said as he shook James's hand.

"And this is Amber," Kris grabbed my hand and pulled me forward. "She's getting her first tattoo today." Kris smirked.

"Hi, James. It's nice to meet you." I shook his hand. "I actually have a tattoo already." I paused as they all stared at me in shock. "It's on my ass," I nonchalantly said. The room fell silent, and Kris and Shawn's jaws dropped open. "I'm joking!" I laughed. "I don't have any tattoos."

The room erupted in laughter.

"So, Amber, do you know what you want?" James asked.

"I‑‑"

"I get to pick this one out," Kris interrupted. "It's a surprise. Do you have some paper? I'll draw it out for you, James."

"Sure, over here." James directed Kris over to the desk. "Amber, you can take a seat in the chair, and we'll be right back."

The three of them were hovering over the desk as Kris drew out whatever this masterpiece of art was going be. They all busted out laughing.

"Kris, can you even draw? I don't like the sound of this!" I yelled over to them.

"I'll have you know I actually draw very well. You'll see." He turned back to his drawing.

I threw my head back against the chair and gazed at the ceiling while I waited. It was covered in art; not tattoo art, but real art. James had a mix of posters and printed replicas of some of the most famous art.

"James? Is that William Blake's *Beatrice Addressing Dante from the Car illustration to Dante's Divine Comedy*?" I asked him in awe.

"Yeah. You know what that is?" James questioned me in shock.

"Yes! I completed my master's not too long ago. I did my thesis on Dante and fell in love with Blake's work. That one is my favorite. That moment when Dante is finally reunited with Beatrice." I sat up and looked at James in shock. "Why... I mean, how do you know about Dante?"

"I know I look rough on the outside, and I make my living giving people tattoos, but I'm an artist. I create art in many forms not just on the skin. I know great art when I see it. That one is my favorite too. Leave it to a woman to guide her man through Hell and Purgatory to set him straight."

We both laughed.

Kris made his way back over. "Don't get him started. He used to be a preacher, and if you get him started, he'll go on for hours." Kris snickered and playfully patted James on the back.

"Here you go." He handed James a small piece of paper, but I couldn't see what was on it.

"And where are we putting this?" James looked at me.

Before I could answer, Kris grabbed my wrist and turned it over, and he gently glided his thumb across the soft, delicate skin, sending goosebumps up my arm. "Right here. I want her to see it as a constant reminder."

"Do I get to see this masterpiece first?" I begged as I tried and failed to grab the paper out of James's hand.

"No. It's a surprise. Just sit back and let James work his magic. Trust me." Kris smiled. His eyes looked so sincere.

"Fine, but only because he has great taste in art." I laid back in the chair. "I trust *you*, James."

James prepped my wrist while Kris and Shawn eagerly waited for the torture to begin.

"How bad is this going to hurt?" I asked. My heart was beating pretty quickly, but I refused to show my fear. I couldn't believe I was actually going to go through with this. I told myself I was going to let go and well, I let go!

"Well, depends on your pain tolerance. This area is pretty sensitive so it might hurt a lot. I'll be as gentle as I can, and it will be pretty quick," James reassured me. "Are you ready?"

"Ready as I'm ever going to be." I took a deep breath and closed my eyes. *You got this, Amber.*

I heard the humming sound of the needle as James grabbed my wrist.

"Do you want me to hold your hand?" Kris asked.

"No. I'm good."

"You sure? Because you're killing that chair's arm and he hasn't even started yet." Kris snickered.

I felt a sudden sharp pain hit my wrist. It hurt, but it wasn't as bad as expected. I loosened my grip on the chair and opened my eyes. "That's it?" I asked. "I'm good. That's nothing." I smirked.

"She's a tough one," James said.

"Yeah, she is," Kris agreed.

I kept trying to catch a glimpse of what James was drawing, but he was holding my wrist in a way that prevented me from seeing what he was doing. The pain dulled and I actually found the humming of the needle relaxing.

Kris pulled out his phone and appeared to be reading a message. He smirked and raised his eyebrows.

Probably his hook up for tonight. My mind immediately went there. Dave used to get the same look on his face when his flings texted him.

"I have to step out for a second. Shawn, wanna join me?" Kris asked.

My heart sank a little. I was having such a good time with him; I guess I forgot who he really was and who I was. My self-doubt returned and consumed me.

"So how long have two been dating?" James asked.

"Who?" I questioned.

"You and Kris?"

"Oh, we aren't dating. Why? Does he bring all his *special ladies* in to see you?" I laughed.

"Actually no. You're the first one, which is why I thought maybe you two were a thing."

"Nope," I sarcastically blurted out. "I just met him a few days ago. I'm a journalist doing a story on The Right Stuff. I'm on tour with them for a few weeks."

"Well, that's too bad. I thought Kris finally found his Beatrice. He could really use a Beatrice in his life." James chuckled and then sighed.

Really? I thought that'd be the last thing he would want.

I heard Kris and Shawn come back in, and they resumed their positions hovering over me.

"How's she doing?" Kris asked.

"Great! You guys are back just in time. I am…" He paused. "Done!"

Kris and Shawn stepped closer, and James showed them.

"Yes! It's perfect!" Kris proclaimed.

"Um, hello! Do I get to see?" I sat up and playfully pushed Kris and Shawn away with my feet since James still had my wrist.

"She's feisty! I like her!" James released my wrist. "I hope you like it!"

I saw a very small, simple, yet elegant piece of art. It was all in black and said "strength" in the most beautiful handwriting I'd ever seen. The bottom loop of the S started with a heart, and the loop of the H ended with an infinity symbol. And around it, just a few little musical notes. *For my love of music.*

"So…what do you think?" Kris asked.

"I actually love it." I continued to stare at it. It was me. He didn't even know me, yet he designed something so perfect for me. My heart fluttered, and I was overcome with emotion. *Whatever you do, Amber…don't cry!* I stood up and gave him a hug. "Thank you. It's perfect!" The feeling of being in his arms at that moment felt so right. The way his big frame wrapped around me as if he was protecting me from the world. I wanted to stay in that moment forever, but it was too much. The emotions hitting me were overwhelming. I quickly pulled away and turned my attention to James.

"James, this is amazing work. Thank you for popping my cherry," I joked. "I will never forget my first." I leaned in and gave him a hug.

"All right, I think it's time to go." Kris grabbed my arm and pulled me from James. He didn't seem amused by my joke. "James, brother, thank you! I owe you one."

I walked away and let them man-hug it out.

"That's a badass tattoo," Shawn said as he watched me admire it. "You know Kris has something similar on his arm."

"He does?" I looked up at Shawn, shocked.

"Yup. It's bigger and more masculine, but same idea."

Kris and James joined us. I looked up at Kris's arm trying to find this tattoo, but couldn't, and figured it must be high up on his arm; hidden by his shirt. *Stupid shirt!*

"Okay, so here are your aftercare instructions." James handed me a piece of paper and a tube of ointment.

"What's the lube for?" I asked as I inquisitively inspected it.

James was laughing. "It's not lube, but I like the way you think! It's to put on your wrist." He paused and shook his head, still laughing. "And I know you're enjoying looking at it, but I need to put this bandage on it. Keep it on there for an hour, then wash it and put this ointment on it. The paper has all the instructions. You'll be fine. If you have any questions, my number is on there, feel free to call."

"She won't need to call, I can help her out. If you need anything, you can ask me," Kris said.

Well, he's being weird. What's his deal?

"Thank you again, James. I'll call if I have any questions." I waved goodbye as I walked out.

Shawn was looking at his phone while we walked to the SUV. "Hey, so Jen wants us to meet her and some of the crew over at this little bar on Fifth Street. They're already there and ordered some dinner for all of us. You guys in?" He looked at us.

"More alcohol. Sure, why not? Sounds like a brilliant idea." I rolled my eyes and got in the backseat. "Do I even have a choice?" I jokingly asked Shawn.

"Nope. You're coming," he said.

"You know I'm in," Kris said as he piled in next to me yet again.

"I was actually a little tired before all that, but I feel pretty awake now. I feel... I don't know, alive!" I shared.

"I think the feeling you're looking for is euphoric. It's that tattoo, I get the same reaction. Feels good doesn't it?" Kris responded.

"It does. I can see why people have a lot of tattoos."

WE ARRIVED AT THE BAR AND IT WAS PACKED. JEN AND SOME OF the crew were spread out among several tables and it was obvious they were already several drinks in, but then so were we. I slid into an open seat next to Jen and proudly showed off my bandage.

"What is that?" Jen grabbed my wrist and peeled off the bandage. "Oh. My. God. You didn't?!"

"I did! Well, actually Kris made me do it, but I'm glad he did. I love it." I beamed.

"Kris! Seriously!" Jen yelled at him.

"What?! She loves it. Don't go all mom on me."

"You don't like it?" I questioned Jen.

"Actually, it's pretty hot. It looks good on you. But Kris is an ass for making you do that," she yelled at him again this time throwing a balled-up napkin at his head. He laughed and ducked as it whizzed by his head.

They were like family. Just watching everyone at the table laugh and give each other a hard time. Just like a family would, and it felt good to be part of it. It's something I'd never really experienced. I felt comforted just sitting there taking it all in.

"What can I get you to drink?" A super attractive waitress

wearing what appeared to be just a bra as a shirt arrived to take our drink orders.

"Can I get a..." I paused to think about what I wanted to continue my drinking bender with.

"Oh. My. God!" she yelled in my ear.

What the fuck?

"Is that Kris August?" She no longer cared about my order and rushed over to Kris. He stood up and gave her a hug. She was jumping up and down and her obviously fake tits were practically spilling out of her bra with every jump. She asked for his autograph, on her tits, and Kris obliged. She was his self-proclaimed "biggest fan." *Weren't they all?*

"You'll get used to that," Jen laughed. "It happens everywhere."

"I don't think I need to get used to it. I'm only here for another few weeks." I chuckled. "I guess I'll just head to the bar to get my own drink. You want one?"

"Sure, surprise me."

"Okay, I'll be right back." I headed to the bar and patiently waited for the bartender's attention. Everyone in the whole place was looking over at the scene the waitress was making, and more ladies started to make their way over for selfies with their favorite band members.

"What can I get you?" a very young, good-looking bartender asked me.

"Give me something fruity. Two of them please."

"You got it." He started to pour in a concoction of items, one of which was tequila. *Yup, it will be another interesting night.* "What did you do to your wrist?" he questioned.

"Oh, nothing. It's a tattoo. I'm pretty badass now," I joked and winked at him. "See." I uncovered the bandage and showed him my new ink. He grabbed my wrist and pulled it closer to get a better look.

"Nice. Beautiful tattoo on a beautiful woman." He turned

my wrist back around and kissed the back of my hand like a gentleman.

I giggled. "Thank you, you're too kind."

"How much does she owe you?" I heard a stern voice ask from beside to me.

I turned around to see who was talking and it was Kris, standing there with his cash in hand trying to pay for my drink.

"Kris what are you doing? I got this. Go back to your lady friends." I shooed him away. "They're waiting and look awfully disappointed." I made a sarcastic pouty face.

"These are on the house," the adorable bartender said as he winked at me.

"No, I got it." Kris threw a twenty at him, grabbed the drinks and walked away.

"Kris, what the hell was that?" I chased after him.

"What? I bought you a drink. You're welcome."

"No, the bartender was buying me a drink."

"No, the bartender was trying to get in your pants." He suddenly stopped walking and turned around to face me. I practically ran into him.

"And that's a bad thing, why?" I grabbed my drink out of his hand and took a sip. "I mean, I know it's been a while, but I'm sure I remember how." I laughed. He didn't seem amused. He just glared at me with those dark eyes. God, those eyes were enough to make any girl's panties wet.

He growled as if he was being tortured. "Just stay away from him."

"I would, but Miss Sign-My-Tits over there is too busy taking selfies with you to take my order. So, I got my own drink. Get over it!" I grabbed Jen's drink from him and walked away.

I handed Jen her drink and reclaimed my seat.

"What was that about?" she asked.

"I have no idea. He's been acting weird all day." I looked over, and Kris was back taking selfies with his entourage, but he still didn't look very happy. He had a smile, but his eyes were giving away his true mood. The eyes don't lie.

"He looks fine to me." Jen laughed. "What is this drink you got me?"

"I have no idea. I asked the bartender for something fruity. It has tequila in it; that's all I know. I think it's pretty good. No?" I took another sip.

"Oh, shit. Tequila again, huh?" She laughed. "Just stay away from Kris this time, and this will be a fun night! Cheers!" She lifted her glass, and I lifted mine.

"Cheers!"

Jen and I had a great time hanging out. We drank and laughed all night, and I even managed to keep my distance from Kris, although I kept catching him watching me. I really didn't know what his deal was tonight.

Thankfully, karaoke was starting, and Shawn and Kris headed up to the stage and were getting ready to perform. All the ladies in the place were crowding the stage because they were lucky enough to be in the right place at the right time and were about to get a free show. Jen and I stayed at the table but had a great view.

The crowd erupted into screams when the beginning beat to *Pony* by Ginuwine blared out of the speakers. Kris and Shawn sang together and danced around the stage. They looked like they were performing in the movie *Magic Mike* with the way they were dancing. I was just waiting for one of them to rip off their shirt or pants and throw them into the crowd of now extremely horny women.

"Hey, I'm getting another drink! You want one?!" Jen yelled at me so I could hear her above the music and screams.

"Sure! Thanks!" I yelled back.

I too found myself mesmerized watching the guys perform

and secretly hoping Kris would rip some of his clothing off. The song came to an end, and all the ladies were cheering for more, but Kris and Shawn were done and trying to make their way back to the table.

An older gentleman came up next and his singing was pretty horrific. Jen had better hurry back with those drinks. I needed one, badly.

"Here you go." Jen reappeared with a few shots.

"Shots again? Really, Jen?!" I laughed. "I think I'm already a bit tipsy and this will for sure push me over the edge."

"Ladies! Is one of those for me?" Shawn asked.

"Hey, nice dance." I smiled at him. "Sure, here." I handed him one of the shots.

"What about you? You need one too." Shawn picked one up and handed it to me.

"No. Shots and I don't mix well." I laughed.

"Come on," Jen said. "Loosen up and live a little."

"Why does everyone think I need to loosen up? I'm a fun girl! People like me, damn it!"

I'll show them!

I picked up the shot, downed it, slammed it on the table and looked at them both. "I'm up next!" I walked toward the stage to pick out my song. They both cheered me on.

"I'm next," I told the DJ.

"What song?" he asked as he handed me the list.

I flipped through a few pages until I found my song. *Possum Kingdom* by the Toadies; a little dark, a little sexy, and I knew all the words. *Perfect!*

The man with the horrible voice was just finishing up. The DJ handed me the microphone, and I headed up.

Holy shit, that's a lot of people. What the fuck are you doing, Amber!

The music started, and the microphone screeched, and I missed the first word, but I caught up quickly. I wouldn't say I was the greatest singer. I usually only sang alone in the car, but I could hold my own and carry a tune. I think I surprised everyone and people started clapping which really got me into it. I started swaying my hips and totally lost myself in the moment. I pulled out my sexiest dance moves. It felt pretty good, but maybe it was the tequila kicking in.

I could see Kris at the edge of the stage, intensely watching my every move. My favorite part of the song came up and when I sang "I'll show you my dark secret," I slowly and seductively unzipped my sweatshirt, took it off and threw it on the ground. Thankfully, I had on a tank top underneath.

The men in the crowd cheered, and I think I even heard a "Take it off!" I smiled and continued my stage seduction; hitting every note perfectly. Toward the end of my performance, a drunk cowboy decided he was going to join me on stage. He came up behind me and started grinding on my ass. I put my arms up and moved along with him. His hands grabbed my hips and started to wander up my body.

Kris suddenly jumped on stage, picked me up, and threw me over his shoulder.

"Hey! I'm not done!" I yelled at him as he carried me off the stage while I was literally kicking, trying to get free. I dropped the microphone causing it to make a loud, horrific noise, but the crowd didn't seem to mind. They were cheering at the spectacle Kris was making. He carried me to the back of the bar to a quiet corner and gently set me down.

I blew my disheveled hair out of my face before flipping out. "What the fuck, August! What was that for?"

He just stared at me and said nothing.

"Ugh! Seriously?" I pushed him away and made my way toward the door. I needed some fresh air. I kicked the door open and stormed out. Thankfully no one was out there except for Donnie, keeping watch as usual.

"Everything okay, Ms. Johnson?" he questioned.

"Yeah, thanks, Donnie. I just needed some air." I kept walking.

"Amber!" Kris yelled after me.

I kept walking. I didn't know where I was walking to, because I didn't have a fucking clue where I was.

"Amber! Stop!" He grabbed my shoulder and spun me around.

"What, Kris?"

"I'm sorry. Are you okay?" He looked at me like a lost puppy dog.

"I'm fine!" I yelled at him. "What did you do that for?"

"I thought he was going to hurt you. I was just trying to protect you."

"Seriously? Yeah, that cowboy hat looked pretty danger-ous! Kris, he wasn't going to hurt me! What the fuck is wrong with you?"

He gently brushed my hair off my neck and rested his hand there momentarily before trailing his thumb down and onto my shoulder, catching the strap of my tank. I shivered at his touch. He was looking at me so intensely. Part of me wanted to fucking take him right there, and the other half of me wanted to strangle him.

"Are you cold?" he asked.

I couldn't answer, I was totally lost in his touch. It was mere seconds, but it felt like an eternity.

"Um, Kris... Sorry, here's your drink." The waitress with Kris's autograph across her tits was standing there with his drink, smiling, waiting for his attention.

"Go back inside. I can take care of myself." I turned around. "Donnie, can you take me back, please?" I asked as I walked away leaving Kris standing there.

I bet she's the lucky winner tonight!

I quickly found the SUV and was impatiently waiting for Donnie to arrive. I was done, and I was exhausted. I just wanted to sleep. I sighed and looked down at my bandaged wrist and smiled, but my heart ached. What was this man doing to me? I rested my head on the SUV door window and closed my eyes.

"Are you ready, Ms. Johnson?" Donnie had finally arrived and unlocked the doors.

"Yes. Thank you, Donnie." As I was getting in, I noticed a woman standing across the street. I paused. She had long dark hair, but it looked like it hadn't been washed in weeks, and her clothing was dirty and tattered. She was a good-looking woman, but she was obviously not in a good place right now. She was all alone and appeared to be watching me. I didn't know anyone out this way; surely, she wasn't looking at me. I turned to see who else was around, but I was the only one there. I turned back around, and she was gone. I climbed into the car and closed the door behind me, eager for my bed.

"Good morning, sunshine!" I heard Jen say as I slowly stumbled into the kitchen.

"Hey," I unenthusiastically said.

"So, what was that last night?" Jen asked.

"You mean with Kris? I don't know. He was acting weird all day." I paused. I needed to change the subject. "Is the arena open yet? I want to grab a quick shower."

"Yeah, it's open. The guys are already setting up."

"Great." I started to walk back to my bunk to grab my things. "Oh, and um, I need to do some laundry. I have nothing left that's clean." I rifled through a pile of clothes, trying to find something acceptable for today. I had one sundress left; that was it. "This is all I have left." I held up the dress and crinkled my nose. I hated dresses. "I don't even have clean underwear; I'm going to have to go commando today." I laughed. "How do you guys do laundry while on the road?"

"Sometimes the arenas will have laundry services, but that's not often, so I usually take stuff to the laundromat or wait until we get a hotel. I'm the lucky person that gets to do all the laundry for the band so, it's usually a whole day thing for me."

"That sounds pretty horrible." I laughed.

"I actually need to do some myself. We can go later today if you want."

"Yes, that would be great. I'm interviewing Kris around eleven, but I'll be able to go after. Does that work?"

"Works for me. Oh, and I found you a room for your interview today. I wrote the details down, and it's on the table," she said as she waved and stepped off the bus.

I showered, grabbed my coffee and navigated my way to the room Jen had found for the interview with Kris today.

Part of me was excited to learn more about him, but the other half of me was terrified. It was just going to be Kris and me alone in a room, and I wasn't sure if my body would behave itself. One touch from that man would throw me totally off track. Plus, I was still confused about his little outburst last night. I wasn't really sure how to act with him after that.

I set up camp in the room early with hopes of getting a little work done. I had never been off my game this much when it came to work. I really needed to focus. I was still working on the questions I wanted to ask Kris, but I couldn't concentrate and found myself daydreaming.

The room I was in looked like it was an old green room suite. It had a few couches, a dining table, and some pretty cool old posters on the wall that appeared to be autographed by previous bands that had played here before. Then I saw one that caught my eye. *Is that The Right Stuff?* I walked over to take a closer look. *It sure is.*

It was a very old poster of the band from back in the early nineties. Each band member had signed it with a little message, and I giggled as I read them.

"No way! I actually remember signing that," I heard Kris say from behind me.

He startled me, and I gasped, "Jesus, Kris. You gave me a freakin' heart attack." I clutched my chest where my heart was pounding.

He laughed. "I'm sorry, I didn't mean to scare you." He looked down at my wrist. "How's it feeling? Can I take a look at it?"

"It's fine. It doesn't hurt at all." I handed him my wrist, and he gently ran his thumb over my tattoo.

"It looks great. I love this on you. You wear it well." He paused and looked up at me. "Are you still mad at me for making you get it?"

"No, I'm not mad about the tattoo. I actually have always wanted one, but for various reasons, I just never got one."

"Really? You've always wanted a tattoo?" Kris tilted his head and raised his eyebrow.

I laughed. "Yes, but today isn't about me. It's about you." I motioned for him to have a seat. I took my seat, and Kris sat across from me.

"Do you mind if I record this?" I held up my recorder.

"Like I told you before, I'm an open book. You have my permission to do whatever you need."

Mmm, dually noted, Mr. August. He looked extra sexy today in his dark jeans and a tight-fitting t-shirt. *Focus, Amber!* Kris was a total jerk last night, yet I was still drooling over him like an idiot. *Something is seriously wrong with me.*

I hadn't exactly been on my best behavior over the past few days either. I took a deep breath. Kris wasn't into me, and

I was not into him. It was time to move on. *Be professional Amber!*

"Great. Let's begin." I started the recorder. "So, can you start by just telling me a little about who Kris August is?"

"Who am I? Good question." He rubbed the day-old stubble of facial hair on his chin as he thought about his response. "Well, I'm forty-three, I was born and raised in Atlanta by a single mom. I have a large family; I'm the oldest of my four brothers and sisters. In fact, you met my sister that day at the hotel."

"That was your sister?" *Huh. I guess I got that one wrong. I'm a jerk.*

"Yup. That was Laura, she's the baby of the family. She came to visit me before I left on tour. I don't get to see my family much these days." He paused as if what he was saying hurt a little. I could see the pain in his eyes.

"My dad left us right after Laura was born, so I really don't know much about him; I was only six when he left. As the oldest son, I always felt responsible for taking care of my mom and siblings. I think that's what motivated me to work so hard. So I could take care of them. There was no greater feeling in the world than being able to buy my mom a house of her own and get her off food stamps."

"Tell me more about your mom."

Kris smiled. "She is the strongest woman I know. My dad was an addict, and from what I understand, he was pretty abusive toward my mom. He was a loser that couldn't keep a job, so she worked three just to keep food on the table. She sacrificed everything for us kids.

"I always had a passion for music, but instruments and lessons were a luxury we couldn't afford, but she always found a way. My first guitar was the oldest, most beat-up thing, but it worked, and I played that thing nonstop." He laughed. "I think I drove her nuts playing sometimes, but she never complained."

He looked up at me. "You actually kind of remind me of her."

"I do? Wow. I mean, she sounds like an amazing woman. Very strong." I looked down at my tattoo and smiled. My heart melted at his kind words. "So, where's your mom now?"

"She never remarried, and I didn't want her to be alone, so once all us kids were grown, and out of the house, I moved her to Hawaii to be closer to her family."

"Is that where she's from? Wait. So that's where you get that dark skin from?"

"Yup. My mom is full-blooded Polynesian, and my dad was white." He paused. "Where does your tan skin come from?"

I sighed. "Well, I don't really know. My mom is white, and I don't know much about my dad. She thinks he was Native American, but I was conceived from a one-night stand... It was the 70s. I never knew my dad." That had always been a painful part of my life that I didn't like to talk about. I took a deep breath and tried to redirect the conversation. I looked at my notes and remembered that I'd never finished writing my questions, so I needed to think of something to ask.

"So, Kris... After the band broke up, most of the members got married and had kids. Why haven't you?"

He looked up at me and laughed. "Well, I guess that's complicated."

"Why is it complicated?" I asked.

"I became famous at a young age. I was a teenage boy that was handed fortune and fame almost overnight. At first, it was overwhelming. I mean, girls would just throw themselves at me and, come on, that's any teenage boy's fantasy, right?" He laughed. "I admit I took full advantage of that in my younger years. But then the band broke up, and they all fell into pretty normal lives out of the spotlight while I chose a different path. I got my first starring role in a movie at the age of twenty-five, and I've been blessed with a very successful acting career ever since."

"That doesn't really answer my question. Many stars get married and have kids. What stopped you?"

"What many people don't understand is how hard it becomes to really find someone. Yes, women still throw themselves at me, but a lesson I learned a little too late in life is they don't want *me*."

"I find that hard to believe." I laughed.

"That's not what I mean. Who wouldn't want all this?" He waved his hands up and down his body and smiled.

"Oh, I get it! They're all turned off by an arrogant guy who's totally full of himself. Makes perfect sense now," I teased.

"Ha! Yeah, I deserved that one." He laughed. "Seriously though, they want Kris August the singer and movie star. They want my money and the status that comes with it. They want the bragging rights to say they slept with someone famous. And you know what? For a long time, I was okay with that. But living that lifestyle took me to a dark place, a very lonely place."

"What about other actresses that are famous too?"

"I have tried to date actresses, but they're just as fake as the others, if not more so. I want someone real who will love me for who I really am, not my name and all that comes with it."

He paused, took a deep breath and looked down at the table. "I know what my reputation is. I own my actions, but that's not who I am anymore. The problem is, that's what people expect from me. The fun, playboy, ladies' man."

I rolled my eyes.

"What? You don't think I'm those things?"

"I didn't say that." I laughed. "I just might add, arrogant and full of himself."

He smirked at me. "Noted." He leaned back in his chair and put his arms behind his head. "My fans are important to me, and they pay a lot of money for those meet and greets, my CDs, my movies; the least I can do is give them my time and let them meet the guy they think I am."

He paused. "But that's not really me. It's just an act."

"You're time? Is that all you give them?" I questioned.

"I don't sleep with them if that's what you're inferring."

"None of them? I find that hard to believe. And is it really all just an act? I always see you with beautiful women on your arm. They're all over you. You're seriously telling me you don't sleep with them?"

"First of all, they're all over me, but I'm not all over them. Have you ever noticed that? And second, my damn publicist insists on setting me up on these fake dates any time I have a public appearance. Those are all fake, an act, that's it."

He stood up, looking frustrated. "Look, I'm not going to say I never sleep with them. I will occasionally meet someone that I think I might want to date. But that's dating, just like anyone else dates.

"Don't you think I want to get married and have kids? I do! Actually, more than anything. And of all the women I have throwing themselves at me, ironically, the one woman that has my heart doesn't even like me."

"Was that Lily?"

"Lily? God, no! How did you ever hear about Lily?" He started pacing around the room.

"Jen told me." I felt weird sitting with him pacing, so I stood up.

"I dated Lily for a short time. She was an extra on one of the movies I was working on, but it didn't work out. She was a partier, and she had an issue with drugs, and that wasn't the scene I wanted to be in anymore. And honestly, I just didn't have feelings for her, so I broke it off. She didn't take it very well and started to stalk me. She was arrested, but instead of allowing her to go to jail, I offered to pay for her to get the help she needed. She wasn't well. Security was alerted a few weeks ago that she left treatment, but no one has heard from her or seen her."

"That's it? Jen made it seem like you did something horrible to her." I frowned.

"Because that's my reputation and I will have to spend the rest of my life fighting that. I get it." He stopped right in front of me and looked me right in the eyes. "Amber, for a journalist you're not very observant."

"What's that supposed to mean?" I defensively asked.

"I was talking about you."

"Me?" I let out an uncomfortable laugh. "What about me?"

"Fuck. I know this sounds crazy." He ran his hands through his hair. "I know it's only been a little over a week or whatever, but Amber, from the moment I met you, you're all I've thought about. But it's pretty obvious you want nothing to do with me."

"I… That…" I didn't know how to respond and was stumbling over my words.

Kris interrupted. "You avoid me and are repulsed by my touch. You can't get away from me fast enough. The other day you even made up an excuse about a bullshit phone call you had to make. I saw you dialing on your calculator, Amber."

Fuck. He did see that.

"Kris, I don't understand. You don't even know me."

"I know it's crazy and I can't explain it myself, but I know enough to see you're smart, funny, genuine, and fucking real! You're beautiful inside and out, Amber." He paused and smiled at me. "And you put me in my fucking place; you're not afraid to give me shit when I dish it out. You don't treat me like some freak on a pedestal, you treat me a like a real person."

He stepped in closer to me, and my heart was beating so

fast I was pretty sure he could feel it from where he was. "Amber, from the moment I met you in that hotel, I knew there was something special about you. When our hands touched, I felt something I have never felt before. And then yesterday when I heard you talking to James about that painting, I knew right then you were the one for me." He started to take off his shirt.

What the fuck! "The one? Kris, what the…"

"Look," he pointed to a tattoo on his back.

I leaned in to get a closer look. *Holy shit...*

"*Lost are we, and are only so far punished,*
   That without hope we live on in desire."

"That's Dante! You…You know Dante?" I stood there staring at the tattoo and gently touched it as if I had to touch it to make it real.

"I met James a few years ago when I was down here filming a movie. I was at a very low point in my life. I didn't have a fucking clue who Dante was at the time, nor did I care, but James knew I needed a little saving and, well, you met James; he's pretty obsessed. He gave me a little life lesson that turned my life around and this tattoo as a reminder. He told me I needed to find my Beatrice to lead me into the light.

"After I straightened up my life, I went back to him a few times. He taught me more about Dante, and I did a little reading on my own, but I will be honest, I didn't have a fucking clue what he was talking about until yesterday. It all just clicked, Amber. You're my Beatrice."

I was in shock. I couldn't even respond to what I was hearing. I wanted to tell him why I ran. I wanted to tell him I felt the same, but I couldn't get the words out.

All of my reasoning, gone. I slowly wrapped my arms around him, and I could feel his heart beating as fast and hard as mine was. I turned him around to face me, and that's when I saw the tattoo on his upper arm that was like the one he gave me. It said "strength" and was embedded in a busy design of musical images.

I looked up at him, and his eyes looked so full of pain. I placed my hand gently on his cheek. Then I let go of any fear I had at that moment, and I kissed him.

His mouth eagerly claimed mine as his hand softly grabbed the nape of my neck, pulling me closer to him. His kiss was gentle, but his tongue was controlling, leaving me powerless and literally buckling at the knees.

He momentarily pulled back, searching my eyes as if looking for permission. "Do you really want this? Because if we start this, I don't think I will be able to stop, ever."

His hand softly trailed down my neck and over my shoulder. His mouth teased my neck as his hands trailed down from my shoulder to the bare skin on my leg where my dress ended. The touch of his hands on my bare skin made me tremble with desire. My clit throbbed for his attention as his hand teased my inner thigh making his way closer, yet always stopping short.

"Then don't stop," I breathlessly moaned.

He softly growled in my ear, "Tell me what you want, Amber. I need to hear it."

I was so lost in his touch that I couldn't speak. I tried, but no words would come out. "Please, Kris," I breathlessly begged.

His hand trailed up far enough for him to realize I wasn't wearing anything under my dress and he groaned as if I was torturing him. "Is this what you want?"

His fingers teased my slick opening. "Fuck, Amber," he moaned as he discovered how ready I was for him. His thumb grazed my clit, and I almost came apart in his arms. It'd been so long since I'd been touched by a man, my mind and body were overwhelmed. I felt my climax building fast. I knew I was moaning loudly and I didn't care who heard me. Every movement of his hand brought me closer to the edge. He teased the entrance of my hot, wet pussy with his fingers and slowly slid inside me, filling the emptiness.

I could feel my muscles tense around his fingers, greedy for more as he slid in and out teasing my clit with every pass. Kris had total control over my body, and he knew it.

He kissed my neck and whispered in my ear, "Cum for me, Baby."

The most powerful orgasm ripped through my body, giving Kris what he demanded. "Oh fuck!" I screamed as I came fast and hard, losing what little control I had left in me. My nails dug into his arms as I tried to keep myself upright. His mouth claimed mine as waves of pleasure rolled through my body.

"Um, Kris?" There was a knock at the door.

I froze in shock. *Shit!*

"Go away!" he yelled then gave me the deadliest, boyish smile I'd ever seen.

"You have sound check in five minutes," the voice from the other side of the door yelled.

"I know!" he impatiently responded back.

He turned his attention back to me and kissed me again like he couldn't get enough. "I'm not done with you," he said as he pulled me in close. I could feel his raging erection pressed up against me. I wanted nothing more than to break it free and finish what we started. "We're going to pick this up again tonight," he continued.

"We'll see," I teased as I tried to compose myself, knowing damn well that this man just ruined me for all other men with just his hands and I wanted nothing more than to continue this later.

"Uh huh. Yeah, we'll see," he grinned. "So, did you get what you needed for the interview?"

I ran my hand through my hair. "Mmm, no I think I'm going to need some more..." I cleared my throat, "time with you to finish this up."

"Meet me in the green room after the show, and we will find someplace quiet," he grabbed my phone off the table.

"What are you doing?" I questioned as I tried to grab it back from him.

"I'm putting my number in." He laughed. He handed me back my phone. "Here." His phone beeped, and he kissed me again before he ran out the door. Then he paused and turned back. "Hey, Amber?"

"Yeah?"

"Why don't you have on any panties?"

I laughed. "Apparently for easy access." His jaw dropped, and he looked at me like he was going to come back and finish the job. "I'm joking, Kris. I ran out."

"Well, tell Jen to take you shopping. I don't want anyone else seeing what's mine." He winked and walked out.

"I'm not—" I began to yell after him but it was too late, he was already out the door.

I sighed and sat down, my legs were still trembling, and I needed to gather myself before I left the room. God knows who is out there or who heard what. I looked at my phone and noticed he had texted himself a message that read: *Thanks for rockin' my world.*

Cocky fucker! I set my phone down, and then it beeped.

Kris: *Rest up, you're going to need it.*

I giggled and smiled at the thought.

Jen and I grabbed some lunch and settled into the laundromat with our cups of coffee and chatted like two school girls while we waited for our laundry to be done. I was so thankful she was on this tour because I would be lost without her.

"So why did I get a text from Kris telling me to take you shopping?" Jen questioned.

"Shopping? Hmm, I don't know. That's weird," I said acting dumb. "I'm good, I don't need anything."

"Well, he has been a pain in my ass about it all day. He told me to give you his credit card and take you to the closest mall. So, I guess we're going shopping after this."

"Jen, please. I really don't want to go. Really, it's—" My phone beeped, and I diverted my attention away from Jen, took a sip of my coffee and checked my message.

Kris: *I can't stop thinking about your tight, wet pussy and how good it's going to feel when I'm deep inside you.*

I choked on my coffee.

"Are you okay?" Jen asked.

I coughed a few times. "Yeah. I'm fine." Flashbacks of him making me cum rushed back to me, making my body ache for him.

"Wow, by the look on your face it must be an interesting message," Jen laughed.

I crossed my legs, hoping a little friction might bring some relief to my now-throbbing lady bits.

"It was just a friend from work. Work drama." I smiled. "Hey, text Kris back and let him know I'm not going shopping. I don't need him to buy me anything."

Jen laughed. "You know he doesn't take no for an answer. We have about an hour until our laundry is done and there's a mall right across the street. I'll make Donnie stay here and guard our laundry instead of us." She smirked. "Plus, I haven't been shopping in forever and would love to go. It's nice to have someone on tour I can hang out with. *Please!*"

"Fine, but I'm only going for you."

"Yes! Let's go." Jen jumped up and headed for the door.

I grabbed my purse and reluctantly followed her. I was going to send a quick response back to Kris but decided to let him stew a little and threw my phone in my purse.

The walk to the mall was a quick one. It wasn't very big and most of the stores appeared to be geared toward more of a younger crowd.

This should be an interesting shopping trip.

Sure enough, the first few stores Jen took me to were wild stores with things I would never wear, but of course, everything looked amazing on her. She was the type of girl that could pull off anything; hence the pink hair.

"Hey, this place looks more my style," I said as we passed a store that looked like it was for adults; not size zero teenagers. Jen followed me in and attempted to help me find something to buy so this trip wasn't a complete waste. The problem was, I hated shopping. I hated everything I tried on.

"What about this one?" She held up a bright yellow dress.

"That's hideous!" I laughed. "I would look like a very large banana. If you haven't been able to tell, I'm very simple and black is my favorite color. There's no way I could pull that off."

She laughed and hung the dress back on the rack. Her phone rang, and she pulled it out of her pocket. "Amber, I have to take this. I'll meet up with you in a few." Jen waved at me as she walked out.

I continued to browse around and came upon the lingerie section. *Hmm. I guess it couldn't hurt to try a few things on.* I picked out a few black lacey items and made my way to the dressing room. I squeezed my triple Ds into a sexy little bra that was nothing more than some lace and wire.

Okay, that's not too bad. Makes the girls look nice!

I turned and checked myself out from every angle. I heard my phone go off in my purse. I dug it out thinking it was Jen looking for me, but it was Kris again.

Kris*: So, did you buy anything yet?*

I decided to snap a picture of myself in the new bra and send it to him.

Kris: *Mmm, baby you look fucking amazing and what about the bottom half?*

Me: *I'm only wearing what you see.*

Kris: *Do I need to come down there and pick some out for you?*

Me: *Nope, I'm good! This morning was so much fun, I might never wear panties again.*

Kris: *You have no idea what you're doing to me right now, do you?*

Me: *What exactly am I doing to you, Mr. August?*

Kris: *I have the worst fucking case of blue balls I think I've ever had.*

Me: *You should probably do something about that.*

Kris: *Where are you? I'll be there in a few, and you can help me.*

Me: *You can't leave, you have a show starting soon. Remember?*

Kris: *They can start without me. I'll quit.*

Me: *You will not! Keep it in your pants. I'll see you tonight.*

Kris: *I can't fucking wait.*

Kris: *Oh and buy some fucking panties so I can tear them off with my teeth later.*

Me: *Doesn't that defeat the purpose?*

Kris: *Then buy a lot!*

I threw my phone back in my purse and finished trying on my items. I was smiling so much, my face hurt. Flashbacks of this morning with Kris came rushing back to me. My body was eager to see what else he had in store for tonight.

I exited the dressing room and hastily grabbed a few pairs

of matching panties before I headed to checkout. *I mean, if he was going to rip them off with his teeth then why not?*

"There you are!" Jen appeared behind me. "Wow, who are those for? And why are you smiling so much?" She paused, "Oh! Amber! Now I know why Kris just texted me to go pay for whatever you were purchasing. Did you guys--"

"No!" I cut her off. "Well...not exactly."

"Amber! I warned you! You're going to tell me everything. It all makes sense now." She shook her head and pulled out a credit card and handed it to the cashier.

"Um, no! I'll pay for this myself," I insisted and handed the cashier my card.

"But Kris said--"

I cut her off again. "I don't care what he said. He's not paying for this."

"Okay," Jen said drawing out that last syllable as she took the card back.

The cashier wrapped up my purchases in pretty pink tissue paper, bagged them up for me and we headed out.

As we exited the store, I noticed what appeared to be the same homeless girl from the bar last night standing off in the distance watching me again. *Am I freakin' losing my mind?* I turned to Jen, "Do you see that girl over there?"

"What girl?" She turned around and searched.

"That one that looks like she's homeless." I stopped walking, turned around, and did a full three-sixty. She was gone.

"I don't see any homeless girl, Amber. Why?" Jen questioned.

"Never mind, my head must be playing tricks on me." We continued our walk back to gather our laundry so we could get to the arena in time for the show.

I looked at my phone and realized how late it was getting. I wasn't sure what time Kris was going to be done, but I knew I needed to wrap up this interview and get to the green room. This woman just wouldn't quit talking about how amazing and hot Kris was. He was her favorite. *Obviously!*

"Who's *your* favorite?" she asked me.

"Huh?" Her question brought me back into the conversation.

"Your favorite band member? Surely you have one."

"Oh, well, they're all pretty amazing." I smiled. *Kris, definitely Kris and his hard...*

"Yes, but Kris is just like the perfect man. I bet he's amazing in bed." She giggled like a school girl.

I'm about to find out if you would shut up!

"Thank you so much for your time. I really need to get going." I smiled, shook her hand and made my escape.

I attempted to make my way through the crowd back to the green room, but it was extra crowded tonight, and no one was leaving. It was as if... Yup, there it was. I could see Kris surrounded by his usual crowd of ladies signing autographs and taking selfies. I stood and watched him flirt, hug and... Yup, kiss his very attractive female fans.

He certainly didn't look like he was leaving anytime soon nor like a guy that was looking to settle down in a relationship. Not that we were in a relationship, but I started to question how honest he had been with what he'd told me earlier.

I pushed my way through the crowd and escaped unnoticed by Kris, making it safely to the green room. I plopped down on the couch and packed up all my stuff.

Fuck! Thirty minutes. I'm waiting thirty minutes, and if he isn't here, I'm jumping in the shower and going to bed. That's it! I refused to be that desperate girl sitting around waiting for a man that stood her up.

I picked up my phone and scrolled through my Facebook, answered some messages and impatiently waited. *Tick tock, fucker!* Thirty minutes came and went, still no Kris. *Ugh! I should have known better! Stupid, stupid, stupid!*

I grabbed my bag and headed into the bathroom, turned on the water, stripped off my dress, stepped in, and washed this day away. All of it!

"Amber? You in there?" Kris pounded on the door.

"No," I responded.

I heard the door open. "I know you're in there, I see your dress on the floor."

"What are you doing, Kris?!" I yelled. "Get out of here. I'm in the shower!"

"I'm so sorry, Amber. I got caught up, and I couldn't get away. I got here as soon as I could."

"It's fine, Kris. You have a life and obligations, you don't owe me an explanation."

"Amber!" He was standing right outside the shower. Only the thin curtain separated us. "Amber, look at me."

I grabbed the curtain to ensure it adequately covered my body, and I peeked only my head out. "What?"

"I do owe you an explanation. You know I would much rather have been here with you. I'm sorry." He touched my face.

"Kris, you don't owe me anything. We fucked around, it's no big deal. I'm fine. Can you go so I can finish my shower?"

"Is that how you see this?" he questioned. "Because that's not how I see what happened. Did I not make myself clear this morning? I don't want anyone else. I'm not just fucking around with you, Amber. I want more. Why is that so hard for you to understand?"

"Kris, I--"

His lips met mine. His kiss was fierce and controlling, and it totally incapacitated any ounce of reasoning or inhibition I had left. He pulled away the shower curtain and slowly backed me up against the shower wall, the water drenching his clothing. I pulled off his shirt while his hands gently explored my body.

"God, you're fucking gorgeous," Kris moaned as he took my erect nipple into his mouth and teased it with his tongue, causing me to arch my back begging for more.

I could feel his bulging hard-on through his soaking wet jeans, begging to be freed. I was unable to stop myself as my hands traveled down his beautifully defined chest and frantically popped the button on his jeans then slid his zipper down.

I glided my hand in and freed his throbbing cock, gliding my hand down the silky skin of his very hard shaft. I quivered with desire.

"Fuck, Amber!" he growled in my ear as he nibbled my earlobe. "I've been thinking about your tight little pussy all day." His voice was rugged with yearning, and heat flooded my core.

His fingers caressed my folds that were drenched with desire, begging for his cock to enter me. He grabbed my arms and pinned them up above my head. I squirmed my hips hoping my clit would find the relief it craved.

"Not yet, Baby." He kicked off his shoes and pants and stood there in front of me looking like a fucking god.

He trailed down my body with his soft kisses. He was down on his knees as the water poured over him. He grabbed my hips and stared up at me; his dark eyes scorching with desire. He looked so vulnerable, beautiful and raw. My heart literally skipped a beat.

His fingers wandered slowly down my leg as he took me with his mouth. It startled me at first. I'd never in my forty years had a man take the time to fuck me like this before.

His tongue danced around my sensitive clit. "Oh, Kris." My

hands dove into his hair, not to control his movements, but to steady myself so I didn't collapse. My legs were weak.

He slid his fingers inside my hot, wet pussy, finding my sweet spot. I was quickly losing myself, I was so close to the edge. This man was a fucking sex god. He knew his way around my body like no one has ever known before.

"You taste so sweet, Baby, I can't get enough of you," Kris said.

The sensation was overwhelming. His fingers claiming my pussy and his tongue giving my throbbing clit exactly what it needed. I came fast and hard. I breathlessly moaned uncontrollably as my body shuddered with each orgasmic wave.

I wanted more. Needed more. "I need you inside me, Kris. Please," I pleaded.

Kris stood up and kissed me. I could taste myself on his lips, and it made me crave him even more.

"Is this what you want, Baby?" He slid his cock in between my legs and teased my tender clit.

"Yes," I whimpered. "Yes, Kris, please," I begged.

"Mmm, I love hearing you beg for me, Amber," he growled as he teased my slick entrance. I thought I was going to cum again right there.

He picked me up, and I wrapped my legs around him, and in one slow thrust, he pushed the head of his huge cock into me.

"Baby, you feel so fucking good," he moaned. With every movement he made, I could feel myself stretch as he dove deeper and deeper until every throbbing inch was buried deep inside me.

"Oh God," I cried out. Taking all of him was the most intense feeling I had ever felt. I could feel my pussy clench around him, greedy for more.

My body trembled as I felt my climax build. His lips kissing my neck, teasing my skin with his tongue, giving me chills despite my body burning with heat. My senses were overloaded; my body tingled. His cock was so hard and claimed every inch of me. With every thrust, I knew he was ruining me for all other men.

I was completely breathless, panting and begging for more as the most intense organism ripped through my body.

"Fuck," Kris grunted as he dove deep into me, slowly grinding as he came hard, violently shuddering.

The feeling of his cock throbbing deep inside me, filling me full of his cum, sent me over the edge again. The most amazing wave of pleasure rolled through my body as I came apart in his arms for the fourth time today.

"Hey, hurry up in there!" Someone yelled as they pounded on the bathroom door.

Kris continued to kiss my neck like he couldn't get enough. "Give us a minute," he yelled back.

I giggled. "We should probably, um…" I was having a hard time finding my words still. "Let someone else use the shower."

"Fine, but I'm not done with you. You're coming back to my bus with me tonight," he demanded as he slowly put me down and slid his still very hard cock out of me, leaving me feeling empty, as if part of me was missing.

"Kris, I don't know about that. I mean Jen––"

Kris cut me off. "I'm not taking no for an answer, Amber. Do I need to beg? Because I will." He placed his hand gently on my cheek, and his lips met mine. The passion between us was undeniable. Whenever he kissed me, it was like nothing else in the world mattered.

"Hurry up!" came an annoyed voice along with another loud knock on the door.

We both laughed, quickly finished our shower and gathered our things.

Kris's clothes were soaked, so he wrapped himself in a

towel. I couldn't stop myself from staring at him as I attempted to get dressed.

Was this really happening? I was lost in thought and struggling to pull up my yoga pants and fasten my bra. I felt like a fucking newborn giraffe; my body was still trembling, and my legs were like two wet noodles straining to hold me up.

My stomach was full of butterflies, and I had a smile on my face that I couldn't contain. My heart was full of excitement, and my body felt all warm inside. *What has this man done to me?* I had never experienced feelings like this before. Was this what sex was really like? Was this what happiness felt like? Was this love?

Surely this wasn't love already, but I guess I wouldn't know what love felt like either. I wasn't sure I had ever been in love or felt love from a man.

This isn't love, I assured myself, this is just sex. *Really fucking amazing sex!* My mind was swirling. Was this what I'd been missing out on all these years?

My butterflies turned into knots, my smile faded, and my stomach churned as emotions washed over me like a ton of bricks.

"Ready, Baby?" Kris asked as he placed a kiss on my cheek. "You okay?" he questioned. He must have seen the panic on my face.

"Yeah. Yeah, I'm good." I forced out a smile. I mean I was good, I was just freaking out.

Kris opened the door, and we walked out. The room was fairly full, and the crew was clapping and hollering when they saw me follow Kris out.

Fuck! They heard it all. Talk about a walk of shame! That was the longest, most unconformable few steps I'd ever had to take following him through the door.

Fuck it. I did a little bow for my audience on my way out.

Yup, I owned it, nothing more to do at this point. The cat was out of the bag and was purring with pleasure!

We continued down the hall to the backdoor of the arena, and it hit me. "Kris, are you walking all the way to the bus in that towel?"

"Yeah, why not?" he questioned.

I laughed. "There are still going to be fans and press out there."

"It's all good. The bus isn't that far away." He snickered as he pushed open the door and made his way out in nothing but a very small towel.

I was right, there were still tons of people beyond the gates, and they erupted with screams. Kris grabbed my hand, and we ran to the bus. Flashes were going off all around us, and all I could hear were women calling his name trying to get his attention, but he didn't stop until we were safely onboard.

His bus was very similar to the one I was on except his was black and gray, more masculine than the purple in my bus and instead of bunks, it looked like he had an actual bedroom in the back. It was surprisingly neat and orderly. I didn't know why, but I'd expected it to be messy. The only mess, however, was a pile of papers on the table next to his guitar.

"Make yourself at home, I'm going to throw something on really quick," Kris said before he disappeared into the bedroom.

I walked over to the table, curious to see what he had been working on. It looked like he was writing a new song. I picked up the top paper, and saw it was titled, "Amber." *Holy fuck, he wrote me a song?*

"You want a drink?" Kris emerged from the bedroom.

"Sure, just some water is fine." I put the paper down hoping he hadn't seen me snooping at his things.

"That's a new song I'm working on. You want to hear it?" He came up behind me and handed me a water bottle.

Busted! "Yes! I would love to." I smiled.

He grabbed his guitar and sat down on the couch. He had only put on a pair of jeans and didn't even take the time to zip or button them up, and there was nothing underneath them either. I took a seat on the couch across from him, mesmerized by how fucking sexy he looked.

"I haven't gotten too far on the lyrics yet, so I'll just play you the music," he said with a nervous look on his face. *That was new*. I'd never seen him be anything other than confident. He looked vulnerable like he was getting ready to bare his soul.

He started playing, and it was absolutely beautiful. It was a slow song, and I could feel the emotion with every chord he played. It was happy yet dark at the same time.

Kris's eyes were examining me for a reaction as he played; they were so dark as if it pained him to play this song. The song was amazing; he was amazing, and at that moment he had my heart. My body ached for him as if he was a drug I needed to survive.

The song ended, and he placed the guitar down. "That's all I have so far. What did you think?"

I had no words. I stood up and walked over to him, and I gently straddled him as he placed his arms around me. I placed my hand on his face and looked him in his stunning dark eyes.

"It was the most beautiful thing I've ever heard." I kissed him. I needed to taste his lips. I could feel his cock hardening beneath me. My thin yoga pants thankfully didn't provide much of a barrier between us. He pulled off my shirt and quickly freed my breasts from my bra, tossing it on the ground as he hungrily sucked on my sensitive nipples, making my core come alive with need. I slid off him, tore off my pants and slithered his jeans down.

His engorged erection was begging for attention. I knelt down in front of him; the head of his cock was glistening with desire. I teased my tongue around his crown before taking him with my mouth. *God, he tasted fucking amazing.*

"Fuck, Amber," he growled as his hand softly pushed my hair back so he could watch me. Our eyes met. Seeing the desire and lust in his eyes made my clit throb. His head rolled back, and I knew he was close. His cock was pulsating in my mouth, ready to explode. His grip on my hair tightened as he moaned and begged me not to stop.

His warm cum filled my mouth as I pumped him for more. His body shuddering as I took in every last drop.

"Come here," he begged as I climbed back on top of him, his hand still wrapped in my hair, pulling me in to kiss him. I could feel his cock still hard and throbbing, teasing my wet folds. I rocked back and forth trying to get the release my body desired, my pussy begging to be filled by him.

"Is this what you want, Baby?" he asked as he grabbed his still very hard cock and teased my entrance.

"Yes. Please, Kris, I need you."

"I will never get tired of hearing you say that," he moaned as I lowered myself on to him slowly taking every inch of him inside me.

His tongue teased my hard nipples as his hands firmly gripped my ass, guiding my movements as I rode him. Our bodies moved perfectly together.

"Damn, you look so fucking sexy, Amber," Kris said with his deep, raspy voice.

My body was on sensory overload. My head felt dizzy, and I felt my muscles tighten around Kris's cock, begging it to never leave. As if he knew what I needed, his hands pulled me into him tightly, allowing me to take him deep inside. I practically came apart feeling him so deep inside me. My body moved and grinded against him, pleading for my release. He gently thrusted, meeting the rhythm of my movements.

"Kris, you feel so good. Don't ever fucking stop."

His movements became harder and deeper, and his grip on me was tight and controlling. It was as if he couldn't contain himself anymore.

The tension in my core built quickly as he pushed himself deep inside me, hitting that spot that desperately desired attention.

I felt myself floating over the edge as pleasure exploded through my body. I shuddered as I screamed his name and moaned for more.

Waves of amazingly strong orgasms rippled through me one right after another. My pussy tightening around his cock, begging for his cum, and his body knew what I needed.

Kris buried his head in my neck as he came deep inside me.

We collapsed and just held each other, content to stay there forever in each other's arms.

I didn't know how much time had passed; I must have dozed off. His arms around me made me feel so safe, and his smell was intoxicating. He eventually picked me up and carried me to the back of the bus. He laid me down and kissed me one last time before we fell asleep.

I AWOKE TO THE FEELING OF SOMEONE RUNNING THEIR HANDS over my forehead and my hair. *Who the fuck?* I was startled, having forgotten where I was and who I was with until I opened my eyes to the most amazing man I'd ever seen.

"Good morning, Beautiful." He smiled at me and kissed my forehead.

"Good morning." I smiled at him. "What time is it?" I looked around for a clock.

"A little after nine. We just pulled in a few minutes ago. You hungry?"

"Wow, I slept really good." I sat up and rubbed my eyes. "Yes. Actually, I'm starving." I could not remember the last time I had slept so well. Was it the amazingly exhausting sex or the fact that I'd slept next to Kris? Either way, it was a win-win!

"I need to go to my bus and get dressed first, though."

"Nope. I already took care of that." He smiled.

"Took care of what?" I questioned.

"I texted Jen and told her to pack up your stuff and bring it over this morning. It's all out front. I didn't want to wake you. You looked like an angel sleeping."

"So, you're moving me in here?"

"Is that okay?" he sheepishly asked. "I mean, I just can't imagine another night without you by my side."

"I guess." I sighed. "But I reserve the right to go back to my bus at any time." I was really a little panicked about this even though I knew it was not living together for real or anything. It was just staying together on a bus for the next two weeks, but it seemed to be moving so fast. *The next two weeks!* Oh God, what happens when my time is up on the tour, and I have to leave? *Pull it together, Amber!*

"Okay, it's settled then!" He smiled with that boyish grin. "Hurry up and get ready. I want to be able to eat breakfast with you before I have my interviews."

I went to get up but realized I had nothing on and my clothes were nowhere to be seen so I improvised and used the sheet as a wrap to cover me.

Kris was watching my every move and taking pleasure in how uncomfortable I was. I walked out to the front of the bus to find my clothes and grab my things. I found everything packed neatly in my suitcase for me. *Jen was amazing!*

"So where do I unpack?" I asked as I rolled it back to the bedroom.

"What's mine is yours. Take any space you want."

"How did you organize all this already?" I asked as I was quickly shoving my clothes into an empty drawer.

"I've been up for a while. I was actually inspired. I finished your song."

"You finished it? Let me see!"

"Nope, not yet. But soon. I promise!"

"Fine," I said with a pouty lip hoping that would sway his decision. It didn't.

I found a pair of the new underwear I'd purchased and slid those on under the sheet.

"Ah, so, you do own panties." Kris came up behind me and shimmied off my sheet, his hands ever so gently grazed my skin, sending chills through me. "God, you're beautiful," he whispered in my ear as he turned me around and kissed me.

I knew I looked like a hot mess, but he didn't seem to care.

"Are you going to get dressed so we can go?" he joked.

"If you would stop distracting me with your magic sex powers I would." I laughed and finished getting dressed as he voyeuristically watched like a hungry animal ready to attack at any minute.

I quickly cleaned up in the bathroom before Kris and I headed out hand-in-hand for breakfast.

"Where are we?" I asked as I stepped off the bus. I had completely lost track of time again. "The mountains are beautiful."

"Colorado," Kris excitedly said. "Oh, and we have plans tonight. We are going out after the show."

"Oh really?" I joked. "So now you're making plans for me too?"

"Well, you are my girl, and I'm not going out without you so… Yes."

"Who says I'm your girl?"

He stopped and playfully swung me around to face him. "Amber, you are my girlfriend, and someday you will be my wife. Stop fighting it."

"Your wife! Kris, I think you're moving just a lit—"

He kissed me, cutting me off, making me melt in his arms and taking away any worry or reservations I had. *How does he do that!?*

"Can we go eat breakfast now?" he asked as he opened the door for me.

"I know what you're doing with your manly sexual powers, Kris August." I stepped inside and continued to ramble. "Trying to manipulate me with your tongue and manly scent and your fucking monster cock. I'm on to your little tricks, Buddy."

"You weren't complaining about my tricks last night, now were you?" He laughed and smacked me on the ass. "Let's go, Princess before breakfast gets cold."

I flipped him the middle finger and smiled sweetly.

"Later, Sweetheart. No worries." He whispered in my ear, "I'll be back in that sweet little pussy of yours again in no time, Baby."

Just the thought made me shiver with excitement. He definitely had magical powers over my body.

"There's the happy couple!" Shawn appeared behind us as we were filling up our plates. "I heard you two had some fun last night. Everyone is talking about it." He patted Kris on the back.

"Seriously?" I laughed. "Is there nothing better to talk about on this tour?" I asked as I gave Shawn a hug. "Are you joining us for breakfast?"

"Yes, I think I will," he said as we walked over to a table

and sat down.

My phone was blowing up in my purse, and I fished it out. Kris's was going off too, but he was ignoring it.

"Oh. My. God!" I said as I opened my text messages.

Julie: *Damn girl! Looks like you're having fun! I want details! Oh, and Rebecca is pissed. Beware.*

Attached were several pictures from last night of Kris and me running through the parking lot with him in nothing more than a towel. It was like every magazine and news outlet was covering the story about Kris August's new "mystery woman." They didn't care that he was in a towel, just about the "mystery woman."

And now I had Rebecca on my ass. I had eight missed calls from her. *Fabulous!*

"Kris, I'm guessing this is why your phone keeps going off." I showed him the pictures that Julie sent. "Let me guess, it's your publicist trying to get a hold of you?"

He picked up his phone and looked. "Yup. it's her. I'm not worried about it, and you shouldn't be either. It's really not a big deal, Amber." He kissed my cheek. "Did you really think you could hide in the shadows forever?"

"No, it's just… It's only been like twenty-four hours! I haven't even told anyone. It's just not how I wanted people to find out, that's all. And my boss is pissed. I'm guessing because someone… No, *everyone* else scooped a story that I should have had an exclusive on." I pushed some cold eggs around my plate, no longer hungry.

"Amber, it will blow over quickly, I'm sure," Shawn tried to reassure me. "Meanwhile, call your boss. It'll be fine."

"Stupid press," I spit out.

"Um, Baby, you do know you *are* the press too, right?" Kris laughed.

"Ugh! Yes, I'm well aware."

"Look, Shawn is right, call your boss. Shit, we can give her a better story tonight if you want?" He smiled a devilish grin and kissed my forehead as he stood up. "I have to get going. Are you going to be okay?"

"Yes. I'm fine, just a little caught off guard I guess." The truth was, I wasn't too worried about Rebecca, I could handle her. I just wasn't ready to tell anyone about us, and now the world knew. I didn't even know what "we" were. I wanted time to figure out if this was a fling or something more before I went and shared with the world and more importantly my son.

It's only been a day. One fucking glorious, orgasmic filled day, but one day nonetheless.

"Come here," Kris grabbed my hand and stood me up. "Text me if you need anything. Promise?"

"Kris, I'm fine." I smiled.

"Promise?"

"Yes, I promise." I rolled my eyes at him.

He kissed me, working his voodoo magic.

"Hey, and don't forget about tonight."

"Are you going to tell me where we're going so I know what to wear?"

He kissed the inside of my wrist where my tattoo was as if to remind me of my strength. "Nope, I have it all taken care of," he said as he walked away.

"That told me nothing!" I yelled after him. *He drives me fucking insane with all his top-secret plans!*

I sat back down at the table and decided to take his and Shawn's advice and do some damage control, but first I wanted to read these articles to see what everyone was saying. I pulled out my laptop and made myself comfy at the table. I wasn't going anywhere for a while.

I typed in "Kris August" in my Google search, and sure enough, that photo was plastered all over. Magazines, news-papers, bloggers, you name it, they all had that photo.

I scrolled through the headlines: *"Who is Kris August's Mystery Woman?" "Is Kris August Off The Market?" "Playboy Kris August at it Again,"* and my favorite *"August Elopes with Groupie."*

Elopes? Groupie?! Seriously! Some A+ journalism right there!

One thing they all had in common is no one knew who I was, so that was good.

I spent some time reading through the articles and laughing at how wrong they all were. My phone rang; it was Rebecca.

"Hi, Rebecca," I answered.

"Amber! I have been trying to reach you all morning, but you were apparently too busy frolicking with the rockstars to answer your phone."

Frolicking? I laughed to myself. "Rebecca, I can––"

"And why does everyone else have this story except for us? I'm really disappointed in you, Amber!" she interrupted.

"Rebecca. They have a story about Kris with some girl, but we have the story on who that girl *is*. You will have your story by the end of the day." I sighed. I cannot believe I'm selling myself out.

"Good point! What about the other story? Are you even getting anything done or just partying?" she spat back.

"I have an amazing story, and it's coming along well. I've interviewed almost all of the band, and I have great testimonials from the fans. I promise it will be great. You have nothing to worry about."

"Well, okay then. I expect that story today at noon your time, wherever you are," she demanded.

I looked at the time, and it was already 11:00 a.m. "Rebecca, no way. That's in an hour. You will have it by the end of the day. No one is going to scoop this before you." I was so done with this conversation. "Goodbye, Rebecca. I need to get to work." I hung up.

Ugh! I slammed down my phone. I could not believe I had

to sell myself out just to make that witch happy. I angrily turned to my computer and started to write my story, but I couldn't. I stared at the blank page, but the words wouldn't come. My stomach churned.

I needed to clear my head. I shut my laptop, shoved everything in my bag and decided I needed to take a walk. I thought I saw a park nearby when I was walking in this morning, maybe I'd head over there. Some fresh air would do me good.

The walk was beautiful. The sun was out, and there wasn't a cloud in the sky. The park was really close, and it actually had a small pond with some ducks and geese swimming around. The view was amazing with the mountains in the background. Very peaceful. I found a bench and sat down and closed my eyes. The feeling of the warmth from the sun on my skin was so relaxing, it melted some of the stress away. At least until my phone went off.

I tried to ignore it, but it went off again a few minutes later. *Ugh! What now!* I picked it up and saw it was Kris.

Kris: *Where are you? I have a break and want to see you. I have something for you.*

Kris: *Amber?*

Me: *I'm at the park next to the arena.*

Kris: *Why you out there?*

Me: *Just needed some fresh air.*

Kris: *I'm on my way. Be there in a minute.*

I smiled knowing he would be with me soon. I didn't want to admit it, but I did miss him, and he seemed to have a way to always make me feel good.

I could see him off in the distance walking toward me; his hands full. Thankfully there were no fans or press gathering yet, or there would have been an outright mob scene.

"Hey, Beautiful!" he said as he sat down on the bench next to me and kissed me on the cheek. "I have something for you!" He handed me a box with a very fancy bow on top.

"What is it?" I asked as I shook the box and smiled at him. "What's the occasion?"

"I don't need an occasion to buy you a gift. Just open it!"

I carefully undid the bow and slid the top of the box off, and inside buried beneath some fancy tissue paper, was a stunning dress with matching heels, clutch purse, and bra and panties. I looked up at Kris and raised my eyebrow.

"It's for tonight. Do you like it?" Kris excitedly asked.

"I do. It's…it's gorgeous," I replied. And it was. It was a casual dress, nothing too fancy and it was black, my favorite color. It was perfect. "I love it. Thank you. How in the world did you have time to get this? And you knew all my sizes!"

"I had some help." He winked at me.

"Of course you did." I laughed. "Well tell your help they did well." I set the box down and scooted closer to him and kissed him. I needed him at that moment more than I needed air. We just sat there in each other's arms, making out like two teenagers that couldn't keep their hands off each other. He gazed into my eyes and his hand gently caressed my hair.

"So, are you going to tell me what's bothering you?" he asked.

I sighed heavily. "Work! I have to reveal myself as your mystery woman in an exclusive story by the end of the day today." I frowned.

"And… You don't want the world to know we're together?" He leaned away as if I punched him in the gut.

"No, it's not that. I just…" I paused. "I'm not the type of person that likes to be the center of attention. I mean, isn't it a bit weird I'm writing a story about myself? That's not who I am. I feel like I'm selling myself out and for what? Kris, it's been like a day. Isn't that a little premature to announce to the world a relationship? And what does this mean for you? What about your people and your image? I don't want to mess any of that up." I was rambling.

"Amber, I can't wait to tell the world about you. I have been looking for you my whole life." He grabbed my hands. "I don't care what it means for my image or what anyone else thinks because this is our life, no one else's. And one of the things I love about you is your modesty and that you're not looking for attention. There's nothing wrong with that, but you're going to be getting a lot of it if you're with me. From me and from the world. I really hope that doesn't scare you away."

He looked at me sincerely with his dark eyes. "And if you don't want to do the story, quit. You don't need that job. I would happily take care of you." He grinned at the idea. "But think of it this way. If you do the story, at least you have control over what it says and how it comes out to the world. It doesn't mean you're a sellout, Amber."

I smiled. "You're right."

"I am?" He seemed surprised.

"Yes," I said as I rolled my eyes at him.

"So, are you doing the story?"

"Yes, I'll do this one, but I'm not going to become an inside source for them on our lives. This one only. If they ask for more, I'm done." I laughed. "And I'm not letting you take care of me. I'll find another job."

"You're talented and smart, and I have no doubt you'll land on your feet, but I will still take care of you whether you like it or not," he teased.

"You're so stubborn."

"Me? You're the stubborn one." He laughed. "So, are you staying out here or do you want to walk back with me?"

"I'll walk back with you. I have a story to write, and I want to get it done before the show tonight." I gathered all my things, including my box of gifts and we headed back.

"I meant what I said about you being talented. I may have

Googled you and read some of your work. You're an amazing writer."

"You Googled me?" I laughed as Kris ran off. It was obvious he was trying to avoid finishing this conversation.

"Hey look, geese!" Kris said all excited like a little kid.

"Yeah, but those little fuckers are mean. I wouldn't get near them," I warned. But it was too late. He was already too far ahead trying to pet one. "Seriously Kris, I wouldn't--"

Kris bent down to pet one, and it snapped at him. "Damn! What the hell?" he yelled. Which got them all riled up and they started to chase him. He was running, waving his arms and screaming incoherently at them, but they kept after him, honking and snapping, trying to bite him. It was hilarious!

"Amber!" he yelled for help.

"Kris, are you okay?" I was laughing so hard I could barely get the words out. "I warned you!" I had tears rolling down my face. I couldn't even walk anymore, I was doubled over with laughter.

"Stay there! I don't want you to get hurt," he yelled as he was trying to fight them off.

"Okay!" I sarcastically replied. "You sure you got this one, Big Guy?" I laughed.

"That was not funny!" he said as he fought the last one off and walked back to where I was still doubled over in laughter.

"Actually, it was hilarious! I wish I would have gotten some photos of that so I could have sold *that* story to the press," I busted out as I wiped the tears from my eyes.

"You wouldn't!"

"No. I wouldn't. I'm just messing with you." I laughed. "Seriously though, are you okay?" I asked as I tried to compose myself. But every time I looked at him, I started laughing again. He had this dead serious look on his face that made me laugh even harder.

He took my box and my bag out of my hands and placed them on the ground. "What are you doing?" I asked. But he just stared at me with that look like he was going to devour me.

"God, I love you," he blurted out as he wrapped his arms around my waist pulling me close to him and kissing me like I'd never been kissed before.

Wait.... Love?

THE REST OF MY AFTERNOON WENT BY QUICKLY. DESPITE having a hard time focusing because Kris dropped the big "L" word on me, I was able to finish my story and get it submitted by the deadline. I also called my son to let him know about Kris so he could hear it from me first and not the press. He seemed happy for me and okay with the situation, which made me feel better.

I had enough time left to shower and get ready before the show. My new dress fit me perfectly and was definitely my style. I was a little nervous because I knew my story would be going live soon on *FAME*'s website and the whole world would know about us. I had a feeling the press would be pretty heavy tonight, so I wanted to at least try to look good.

I was looking forward to spending the night out with Kris. I hadn't seen him since this afternoon, and that last kiss left me craving more of him. I heard the music start, so I packed up my things and headed out to my usual spot side stage.

It was another sold out show and the noise level, as usual, was deafening. I put in my earplugs with hopes they would help. Donnie nodded at me to acknowledge my arrival, and I waved back at him as I settled into a folding chair he had put out for me.

The concert was the same show they put on every night, but I was still glued to every move as if it was the first time I saw it. As they neared the end of their last song, I got up to make my way backstage, but then Kris went off script. I stopped, curious as to what was going on.

"Thank you for coming out. I have something special to share with you all tonight." The crowd went wild, and I sat back down. "I have a new song that I just finished, and you'll all be the first to hear it. I was inspired to write this song by someone very special to me. Amber, Baby, this is your song."

He sat down on a stool with his guitar and started to play. I recognized the melody, and my heart fluttered as the crowd erupted. His voice was sexy and rugged as he sang the most beautiful love ballad I had ever heard. I could see the place light up as the crowd held up phones and waved them back and forth. I giggled as Kris's eyes met mine. This man had my heart and my soul. This was new territory for me, but this was real. *I loved him too.*

The concert ended, and the guys rushed off stage. I ran back there to find Kris. When I spotted him, I ran over to him and jumped in his arms. He looked so fucking sexy and was dripping in sweat, but I didn't care. I needed him.

"Hey, Beautiful." He welcomed me in his arms.

I couldn't even speak, I just kissed him. The passion and love I felt for this man was so strong that I couldn't even express it with words. In fact, I was not even sure if I knew how to say those words to a man.

My heart raced as adrenaline pumped through my body; I was terrified at these feelings I was having. It was all so new. I pulled away from our kiss and looked him in the eyes. "I love you, too."

He carried me to a nearby room and slammed the door behind us. He kissed me deeply, his tongue mingling passionately with mine.

"Say it again," he begged.

"I love you, Kris." I moaned as I eagerly unzipped his pants and pulled out his manhood. I greedily slid my hand up and down his rock-hard shaft.

His hand traveled up my dress, and in one swift movement he tore off my panties. We were like two teenagers that couldn't get our clothes off fast enough. His fingers teased my swollen, slick folds.

"You're soaking wet," he said in a sexy, raspy voice.

His palm grazed my clit as his fingers dove inside me. His touch sent all the air out of my lungs.

"Fuck me, Kris," I demanded. My words surprised me, but I couldn't stand another second without having him inside me. I didn't need foreplay, I just needed him, buried deep inside me. He lifted me up and set me on a nearby table and positioned his cock at my entrance, ready to claim my wet and ready pussy. My pulse was thumping beneath his lips as he kissed my neck.

"Is this what you want?" he asked as he teased me with just the tip of his engorged cock.

"Yes," I barely got out, my breath hitching in my throat. "Please!"

"Please what?"

"I need you inside me."

Kris slowly and torturously slid his cock inside me. Making sure I felt every bit of him. "This is all yours, Baby. No one else's," he said as he started to thrust ravenously deep inside me.

"Good God, woman, you have no idea what you do to me," he moaned in my ear, sending chills through me.

He took me quick and hard as we feverishly lost ourselves in each other. It was sheer ecstasy. His grip on my ass was tight as he pulled me closer and closer to him and he drove deeper and deeper into me with every push.

My fingers dug deep into his back as I begged for more. "Kris, that feels––"

"Fucking amazing," he said finishing my thought. His mouth crashed onto mine.

I loved the way he kissed me, so full of desire and need. I wanted to scream out, but I knew there were people just outside the door. I had to bite my lip to keep from crying out as my release came hard. Again and again, wave after wave of desire ripped through me.

We just laid there as we caught our breath.

He picked my tattered panties off the ground and put them in his pocket.

"Well, those didn't last very long." I giggled.

"Mmm, no and that dress is next. You look amazing."

"Hey now! At least wait until later to rip the dress off," I joked as I put myself back together.

"No promises." He smiled. "We should get going, I want to clean up before we head out. The car will be here soon."

"Yeah, I might need a few minutes too." I laughed. I was sure I was a mess, but it was worth it.

We walked toward the door. He paused and turned to me. He gently brushed my hair out of my face and kissed me so tenderly. "I love you too, Baby."

WE PULLED UP TO WHAT LOOKED LIKE A FANCY NIGHTCLUB. THE line was wrapped around the building, and the press was out in force. The cameras were going before we even opened the door. *Deep breath, Amber, and don't fucking trip!*

"You ready?" Kris asked.

"As ready as I'm going to be," I sighed. "So, what is this place?"

"It's a new club that is having their grand opening tonight, and I got us all a VIP table," Kris said.

"That's a lot of press," I said as I stared out the window.

"Amber, you do know that you are the press, right?" Brad joked.

"Yes, but now I'm on the other side of it and it's intimidating," I replied.

"It's not as bad as it looks," Brad laughed. "You'll get used to it."

"Well, I'm thankful to be able to attend with you all tonight. Thank you for letting me tag along." I hadn't spent a lot of time with the whole band, so I really was looking forward to hanging out with them and getting to know them better.

The door opened, and Kris grabbed my hand as he stepped out, pulling me out behind him. The flashes from the cameras were blinding. The people in line started screaming as they saw Kris and the rest of the band exit the limo. Kris squeezed my hand to reassure me as if he could feel me panicking.

We started to walk toward the door, but the press swarmed. Donnie was in front of us trying to clear a path, but microphones and cameras were being shoved in our faces.

"Kris, are you and Amber serious?"

"Amber, are you and Kris getting married?"

"Kris, does this mean you're off the market?"

Questions were being yelled at us from all directions. I just smiled and held on to Kris as he led me through the chaos into the safety of the club. The rest of the band was still outside signing autographs for the fans waiting in line.

We were escorted past the bouncers to a private seating area in the corner of the club. It had a red velvet curtain that you could pull around the area for privacy. The table had an ice bucket with a bottle of Cristal champagne and several glasses ready and waiting for us. It was surrounded by a few velvet-covered chairs and a plush couch fit for a king.

The club was packed, and the music was loud; the bass vibrated through my body. It was a little quieter at the table so we could at least hear each other talk. "Holy shit! That was more than I expected. I guess the story got released," I said to Kris.

"I think you're right and it's time to celebrate!" he said as he poured us each a glass of champagne. "To us!"

"To us!" I repeated as we clinked our glasses together and took a sip.

To us? Wow. Are we really an "us"? I didn't know why but just hearing that made me freak out a little. The feelings I had for him were so strong, and everything was moving so fast I struggled at times to process that this was really happening. It was surreal.

Kris pulled me to him. "Thank you."

"You're welcome?" I questioned. "What did I do? I should be thanking you." I laughed.

"For finally showing up in my life after all these years and for making me the happiest man in the world. This is just the beginning of something great. I can feel it," he said.

"I guess I just got a little lost along the way. Thank you for finding me." I leaned in and kissed him.

"Get a room you two!" Brad yelled as he arrived at the table with Shawn and Jason.

"I see you guys started without us." Shawn laughed as he poured himself a glass of champagne.

The velvet curtain was open, so we could see all the action in the club. Thankfully they were not allowing the press in tonight, but that didn't stop people from constantly snapping pictures with their phones. *Yeah, I'm not sure I'll get used to that.*

A tall, thin, yet well-endowed woman in a short black skirt and white, see-through tank top arrived at the table. "Hello, gentlemen! My name is Traci and I will be your server tonight. Just let me know what I can do for you."

Of course, she ignored me and placed her hand on Kris's

arm, "I'm a huge fan, Kris. If there is anything you need, please let me know."

I rolled my eyes as she stressed the word *anything,* as if I didn't know what she was implying.

"Amber, do you want anything?" Kris asked me as he pulled his arm away from her touch.

"No, I'm good with this for now." I held up my glass, smiled and kissed his cheek as if claiming my territory.

"We're good," he said to Traci and then grabbed my hand. "Let's go dance."

We navigated our way through the crowd and found ourselves a spot on the dance floor. It was dark with just the flashing of the lights that went along to the beat of the music. I noticed Donnie wasn't far behind us just in case things got out of control. The music changed to a slower, rock song; *Change* by the Deftones. Kris pulled me close, and everyone else faded away; it was like we were the only ones on the dance floor.

I could feel the music vibrating through my body as we swayed, our movements becoming one. His lips teasing my neck, his hands seducing my body, my sensuality coming alive. Adrenaline rushed through me as my heart raced from excitement, lust... and love.

In such a short time, he had transformed me into a version of myself that had laid dormant for years, and it felt liberating to finally find myself. He was making me a better person, a stronger person. One that didn't fear, one that could love and be loved, one that was finally comfortable in my own skin. I felt like with him by my side, we would conquer the world. I was no longer that empty shell I once was.

This man had the power to make me the happiest woman alive or totally crush me, but it was worth the risk. Love was worth the risk. Wasn't it?

Donnie approached us and said something in Kris's ear. Kris nodded.

Kris leaned into me. "I have to go meet the owner really quick. You want to come with me?"

"No, I'm good," I yelled. "I'm going to use the ladies' room and grab a drink."

"I'll meet you back at the table in a few minutes," he said as he gave me a quick kiss. He walked away and made a head gesture to Donnie, telling him to stay with me.

I really wished he wouldn't do that. Kris was the one that needed security, not me.

I fought my way through the club to the ladies' room, and of course, there was a line, but thankfully it wasn't too long. Poor Donnie, I was sure he was just thrilled at having to watch me in line for the bathroom. I gave him my best "I'm sorry" smile.

"Hey aren't you Kris August's newest fling?" A very drunk girl stopped on her way out of the bathroom.

"Excuse me?" I asked.

She turned to her friends. "That's her. That's the girl in the picture." She turned back to me. "I don't know what he sees in you. You're not even his type. I mean you're fat and not even hot," she blurted out.

"And you would know what his type is?" I questioned.

"Yeah, I'm his type," she said as she adjusted her bra to ensure more cleavage was showing. She leaned in closer to me. "I'm going to fuck your man tonight."

I laughed. I could see Donnie coming closer and I waved him off to let him know I was fine. I didn't even know what had come over me, but I grabbed her by her fake hair. "If you even so much as look at Kris tonight, I will rip this weave off your head and make you eat it." I gave it one more tug to make sure I got my point across.

She just looked at me in shock, while her friends all came

to her rescue. They were yelling and calling me names while they comforted their friend.

Donnie rushed into the scene and pushed the girls away from me. "You okay?" he asked me.

"Yup. I'm great!" I smiled as I pushed past the girls and walked into the bathroom. *Bitches!*

I arrived back at the table a few minutes later, but no one was there, so I decided to head over to the bar to grab a drink since I knew Traci wasn't going to show up unless one of the guys occupied the table. The bar was packed, and I stood there for several minutes, failing to get the attention of the all-female bartenders.

"Here, let me," the guy standing next to me said. He held up his money and simply nodded at one of the bartenders, and she came running over.

"Seriously!" I laughed. "I've been trying forever to get their attention."

"Ladies first." he smiled.

"Thank you." I turned to the bartender. "Can I have a tequila sunrise with Patron, please? Make it a double."

"Whiskey on the rocks please," he told the bartender before she hurried off to make our drinks. "I'm Scott," he said as he held out his hand.

"Amber," I shook his hand as the bartender arrived with my drink. I handed her my money, but Scott stopped me.

"This one is on me." he smiled.

"Thank you, but I got this." I handed my money back to the bartender as Kris headed my way.

Scott placed his hand on my shoulder and leaned in. "I—" he started to talk but froze as Kris arrived. He removed Scott's hand from my shoulder, picked me up, and carried me away.

"Hey! My drink!" I yelled.

"I'll get you a new one," he said as he playfully slapped my ass.

"Put me down. I can walk!"

"Nope. I don't want any more guys flirting with my woman," Kris said as we passed by the group of the girls from the bathroom incident. Their jaws dropped, and I flipped them off. He carried me all the way back to our table and set me down and closed the velvet curtain.

"So, I heard you a had a little incident?" He flashed me his devilish grin.

"Nope. No incident." I smiled, crossed my arms and acted all innocent. "I just put some drunk bitch in her place. How about that drink?"

He poured me another glass of the Cristal. "So, what did she say?"

"It doesn't matter. It's over." I sipped my drink hoping he would change the subject.

"Amber. Tell me."

"Fine. She said I wasn't your type and called me fat and ugly and said she was going to fuck you tonight." I sipped my drink. "So, I pulled her fake ass hair and told her I would make her eat it if she even looked at you." I giggled.

"What the fuck? You know that's not true, right?"

"Yeah, I guess. I just... I don't know." Truth is, I really didn't know. Deep inside I still had lots of doubts about us.

He kissed me. "Amber, I'm actually really fucking turned on right now knowing you did that. In fact, I really wish I would have seen it, but you cannot go around doing that to the fans. They're going to say some messed up shit, but you have to learn to ignore it and know it's not true." He grabbed my hand and placed it on his rock-hard package to show me how turned on he really was. "That's all for you, Baby, and that is never going to change."

"I know. But, um...you also can't keep picking me up and carrying me away any time a guy even talks to me."

"Why not? I don't like seeing other men gawking at you."

"And I don't like other women talking about fucking you. It makes me want to pull out their weave and shove it down their throat."

"Noted." Kris laughed. He pulled me close and wrapped his arms around my waist. "I think we need to finish our dance still."

"Yes, I think you're right," I said as we slowly swayed backed and forth despite the fact that the music was fast with a heavy beat. We just danced, gazing into each other's eyes as the rest of the club around us disappeared.

"I'm sorry I threatened one of your fans," I said, and I unzipped his pants and slid in my hand. "But you need to also trust me that I love you and I don't want any other man."

"Mmm," he moaned at my touch. "I know." He kissed me and pulled me closer. "I love you too, and I'm sorry. I've just never felt so strongly for anyone in my life, and I don't really know how to control myself. I'm learning."

"I feel the same way. This is new for me too," I said as I freed his erection from his jeans.

"We're more alike than you think. Never been in love, never been loved," he said as he slid his hand up my dress. Staring intensely into my eyes.

My heart raced, and his fingers teased my swollen clit. "What if someone walks in," I breathlessly asked.

"I don't care who sees us, Amber. I want you now," he growled. He backed me up and laid me down on the plush couch. His engorged head entered my wet and hungry opening.

"Mmm, Kris," I moaned. There was something thrilling about the idea of someone seeing us. He brought something primal out of me. My need for him was so strong my inhibitions melted away.

With every thrust, he made his way deeper and deeper inside me until I had all of him. His movements were controlled and quick, searching for his release. His eyes were closed as if he was completely lost in me, his rhythm matching the hard bass of the music, which I could feel vibrating through my body, adding to the pleasure. My senses were on overload. Every stroke driving me insane with need.

"Knock, knock. Can I get you--" Traci walked in. "Oh, God. I'm so--"

"Get out," Kris snapped at her.

She dropped her tray sending drinks crashing to the ground as she exited, but Kris didn't miss a beat, and I was so close to coming I begged him for more. He grabbed my ass and pulled me into him, allowing him to dive even deeper inside me, sending me over the edge.

I violently shuddered as my orgasm sent waves of pleasure through my body over and over again. The music was so loud it drowned out the sounds of my pleasure.

"I love watching you cum," he grunted as he continued to claim me, on a mission to make me cum again. He lifted me off the couch and turned me around. He swept my hair off my neck as he bent me over the table and entered me from behind. His hands trailed down my back before resting on my hips.

I felt my pleasure build again, and I ached for another release. Kris's hand wrapped around and softly teased my tender clit.

"I'm going to cum so fucking hard. Cum with me, Amber," he begged. I felt his cock release deep inside me as my body obeyed and came again with him. My legs trembled, and I could barely hold myself up. I was thankful for that table under me.

We just laid there for a few minutes, neither one of us wanting to move or break contact. We heard the guys close by so Kris quickly helped me up and pulled my dress back down before putting himself back together.

"I just can't get enough of you," Kris said as he embraced me in a heated kiss.

"What the fuck happened here?" I heard someone say just beyond the curtain.

Brad, Jason, and Shawn arrived back at the table. "Seriously, you two!" Brad joked. "What's with the broken glass?" he asked as we all stared down at the mess on the floor.

Kris and I just laughed and shrugged our shoulders. "I have no idea, dude," Kris replied.

"Whatever. Hey, if you two are done, we need to get going. The buses are leaving soon, and we need to get back," Brad said.

"I'm ready, I just want to use the restroom before we go. I can meet you guys at the car," I said as I grabbed my clutch off the chair.

"I'll go with you," Kris said.

I rolled my eyes at him. "Kris, I can go by myself."

"Fine, but no more hair pulling." He laughed. "And Donnie will be near if you need anything."

"Wait, there was hair pulling, and I missed it?" Shawn asked.

"Yup. My lady can kick some ass, so you better watch yourself," Kris joked.

"You got in a fight?" Shawn asked me.

"No, I just put a bitch in her place." I smiled. "I will see you all at the car." I made my exit.

"Oh damn! You have to tell me this story," I heard Shawn say as I walked away.

The wait for the ladies' room was thankfully much shorter this time, so I was able to get in and out quickly. I stepped outside, and the air felt refreshing. It was so hot inside the club, and the breeze felt amazing. I stood there for a second to cool off.

"He doesn't love you," someone from behind me quietly

said.

I turned around, and there was a woman standing in the shadows on the side of the building. I couldn't quite see what she looked like. I really didn't want to get into it with another fan, so I started walking away.

"Did you hear me!" she yelled.

I stopped and took a few steps in her direction. "Do I know you?" I asked.

She took a step toward me, coming out of the shadows so I could see her. It was the homeless girl I saw in Texas. *How can this be?*

"He'll hurt you," she whispered.

Her voice gave me the chills. I looked around; I knew Donnie had to be close by. I spotted him walking my way. I turned back around to confront this girl, and she was gone.

"Everything okay, Ms. Johnson?" Donnie asked.

"Yeah, I just…" I paused. "There was a girl…" I didn't even know what to say. "I think I saw her in Texas." I rubbed my head. I was so confused.

"Groupies," Donnie said. "They travel with the band from city to city. I wouldn't worry too much about it. They're generally harmless. Just get a little aggressive sometimes."

I sighed. "Okay."

"This way, Ms. Johnson. The limo is waiting."

OVER THE NEXT FEW DAYS, KRIS AND I WERE INSEPARABLE. Every chance we had, we were by each other's side, making the most out of the time we had left on tour. We even started writing a song together. I wrote the lyrics, and he wrote the music.

Life was good, and I felt so alive. I was experiencing so many things for the first time in my life. It was like Kris woke me from a forty-year slumber. I was dreading the day it all came to an end. We hadn't really talked about what happens when I had to go back to Chicago, but we both knew it was coming quickly.

I felt the bus come to a stop and turn off; we must have arrived in Portland. It was still dark outside; there was no sunlight at all. I could hear the rain steadily tapping against the window. It was one of those days that I would have loved to stay in bed all day, but I was actually looking forward to today. The band had a day off, and Kris was flying me someplace for a surprise date.

As usual, he was already awake, and I could hear him playing his guitar in the front of the bus. I got up, got myself dressed and cleaned up in the bathroom before making my way out to him.

I could tell something was off with him. He looked sad and lost. I'd seen that look before when I was watching him play back in Texas. He was so deep in thought that he didn't even notice I was in the room.

"Hey. Everything okay?" I asked.

It was like a light switch flipped in him. "Hey, Baby! You're up!" He smiled and put down his guitar and came over to kiss me. "All is good now that you're here."

"What time are we leaving?"

"The car will be taking us to the airport in about an hour, and you need to pack because we won't be back here tonight." He winked.

"I don't even know where we're going or what we're doing, so what do I pack?" I joked.

"Just pack the basics, and I'll take care of the rest."

The rain appeared to be letting up, and I could see that there was a Starbucks across the street. I was dying for a peppermint mocha. "Okay, but I'm going to run over to Starbucks really quick and get a coffee. You want something?"

"I'll have Jen get it for you," he said. "You don't need to be out there right now."

"Kris, that's silly. It's right across the street. I'll be right back."

"Amber, you can't go," he said firmly.

"Excuse me? I can't go? Since when do you get to dictate what I can and can't do?" I was so confused about where this was coming from. "It's just coffee across the street, Kris. I'll be right back." I grabbed my purse and headed for the door.

"Amber! Just trust me for once," he snapped at me.

I walked out. *What the fuck is wrong with him?*

"Amber!" He ran after me. "Please get back on the bus. Damn it! Why are you so stubborn!" He grabbed my arm, "Stop!"

"Stubborn?! I'm the stubborn one?" I yelled at him. "Kris, this is ridiculous. What is going on with you?"

He just stood there and stared at me as he often did. He looked like he wanted to talk but couldn't find the words. The rain started again. "Can we please go back inside, it's raining," he said.

"No, not until you tell me what this is all about."

"I can't," he pleaded.

"Then I'm going to get coffee." I took off walking.

"Okay, fine!" he yelled. "Please stop."

I stopped, turned to face him and waited for him to tell me what was going on. He was already soaking wet from the rain; his white shirt was clinging to his body. He ran his hand through his hair, pushing it out of his eyes as water dripped down his face. I could see he was distraught. Part of me wanted to comfort him, but the other part of me was pissed for the way he was acting.

"Security received some threats last night." He paused. "We're not sure how real they are, so they're looking into them, but they knew some things about me and are threating to go to the press."

"What things? And since when are you worried about what people think of you?" I asked.

"Amber, you know I was in a dark place for many years, and I did things I'm ashamed of. The only person I care about what they think of me is you. I don't want you to leave me."

He pushed his soaking wet hair out of his face again, and I could see the panic in his eyes. "And now I'm being punished. I finally get my shit together and find happiness and the world wants to take it away. They want to take you away."

He looked around as if to make sure no one was watching, "I don't care what they release about me, I can handle that, but Amber, the threats are against you. People want to hurt you to get to me." A tear rolled down his face. "I could never live with myself if something happened to you. I'm just trying to protect you. I'm sorry, I didn't want to tell you because I didn't want to burden you with my baggage."

I stepped closer to him. "Kris, I don't want you to feel like you have to hide things from me. I want to be here for you, baggage and all. Shit, I have baggage and a lot of it. Look, I may not know all the dirty little details of your past, but I know who you are now and you're a good man. While I hope that someday you'll feel comfortable sharing these things with me, you need to know that your past will not change the way I feel about you." I paused. "Wait, you didn't kill or rape anyone did you?"

He laughed. "No, nothing like that."

"Oh, thank God!" I laughed. I placed my hands on his soaking wet face. "You have to learn to trust me too. We are in this together. I knew what I was getting into when I started dating you, Kris. It may have scared the shit out of me..." *Still does!* I looked straight into his beautiful dark eyes. "But you're worth it." I smiled. "We are not going to live in fear. We are going to go get some fucking coffee and then change into some dry clothes and get ready for our flight. Okay?"

He sighed and smiled. "Okay."

"Great!" I started to walk, but he grabbed my arm and pulled me to him.

"I love you more than you will ever know," he whispered right before he kissed me.

We stood there in the pouring rain in each other's arms, lost and in love.

———

"ARE YOU GOING TO TELL ME WHERE WE'RE GOING YET?" I excitedly asked for the tenth time since we'd taken off. I had never been on a private plane before, and I felt completely spoiled. The leather seats were very large and extremely comfortable. They were situated so Kris and I could sit facing each other, only a small foldable table separated us. It was just Kris and me; the security team, which was larger than usual, was upfront.

"I'll give you a hint," he said as he reached into his bag and pulled out a blue box with a little white bow on it. "Here. Open this." He smiled.

I untied the bow, and slid it off, and lifted the lid off the little blue box. Inside was the most beautiful white and black diamond necklace, bracelet, and earring set I have ever seen. I gasped. "Kris, this is beautiful, but…" I paused as I was taken by their beauty. "It's too much. When would I ever wear something like this?"

"Well, I'm hoping you'll wear them tonight."

"Tonight? I didn't pack anything that is fancy." I looked up at him.

He was smiling. "Our first stop is to get you a dress for tonight. No worries, Baby. I told you I have it all covered."

I unbuckled myself and sat on Kris's lap. I wrapped my arms around him and kissed him. "Thank you. You're an amazing man. You know I don't need all this, right?"

"I know, but it makes me happy to spoil you. I want to do these things for you," he said as he wrapped his arms tightly around me, pulling me closer.

I smiled. "Where have you been all my life?"

"Right here waiting for you to save me." He kissed my forehead.

"I saved you?" I questioned. "I think you saved me. I thought my life was okay before I met you, but now I see how much I missed out on and that I was in such a dark place. Kris, you brought light into my life like I've never experienced before. You make me want to enjoy my life again."

"Baby, I was so lost before I met you. You're my Beatrice. You're guiding me from the darkness into the light. Every day you make me into a better man." His hand gently embraced the back of my neck, and he pulled me in for a kiss, his tongue passionately with mine as we just enjoyed each other's kiss and embrace, losing all track of time.

A loud crackling sound came through the speakers snapping us back into reality. The captain cleared his throat. "Seems like we're coming into a little rough air up here as we approach Los Angeles. I'm going to ask that everyone take their seats and buckle up. We should be on the ground shortly."

"I don't want to go back to my seat," I whimpered as I slid my hand over Kris's very hard erection that was begging to be freed. I wanted Kris to take me right here on this plane. My body was just as ready as his. Kris moaned at my touch. He removed my shirt as his fingers teased my sensitive nipples, his lips kissing my swollen breasts. I popped the button on his pants and was working on the zipper when the plane suddenly dropped.

If it weren't for Kris's firm hold on me, I would have been airborne. "Yup. Time to get in my seat," I said as I quickly made my way back to my seat and pulled my seatbelt tight across my lap. My shirt was still on the floor, but I didn't care.

"Fucking turbulence," Kris growled. He looked like a pouting child.

"So, Los Angeles, huh?" I excitedly tried to divert our attention, but Kris just stared at me with heat in his eyes. The plane continued to bounce and I quickly realized so did my exposed breasts.

"Um, Kris? You in there, buddy?" I teased. No response. *Okay I can have a little fun with this.* I reached around my back and unhooked my bra and slowly slid it off, exposing myself to him.

"God your body is so perfect," he moaned as he uncomfortably shifted in his seat; his hand trying to reposition his tender erection.

I could see that we were close to landing and we didn't have too much longer. Thank God because I was about to combust if I didn't have him inside me soon.

Kris picked up his phone and appeared to send a quick text. He then folded the table between us back into the wall. "Unbutton your pants."

I did as he instructed. Curious as to what he had in mind.

He reached down, lifted up my legs and pulled my jeans off and threw them down on the floor next to my shirt and bra. "That's much better," he said as he reached in his pants and freed his cock; the tip glistened with pre-cum as his thumb ran circles around it.

I wanted nothing more than to consume him with my mouth. I licked my lips with desire as his hand slid up and down his shaft; teasing me. My pussy was jealous with envy, aching to do that for him. My clit was throbbing, begging to be touched; I couldn't wait. I slithered my hand in my panties and slowly pleasured myself as Kris watched.

"Fuck, Amber. You're killing me," he growled as the plane touched down on the ground.

"Thank fucking God." The plane began to slow, and he ripped off his seatbelt. "Come here," he demanded as I undid my seatbelt and stood up to meet him.

His hand dove down my panties, "Can I help?" he asked as his fingers slid into my drenched pussy.

"Kris," I begged as he laid me down on the bench seating; pulling off my panties and taking my nipples in his mouth. His cock teased my begging entrance; my whole-body quivering with need.

"Is this what you need?" he asked as his engorged head penetrated me.

"Yes," I moaned. He always felt so fucking good inside me, and always gave me exactly what I needed. Multiple times!

THE CAR PULLED UP TO A VERY FANCY HIGH-RISE BUILDING.

"Where are we?" I asked. "I thought we were going shopping?"

"I live here. Well, one of my places. I brought the store to you." He smiled.

"One of your places? How many places do you have?" I asked.

The car door opened and Kris stepped to the curb and offered me his hand to help me out. "I have four."

"Four!" I yelled. "You have four homes."

"Yes. I travel a lot for work and will spend long periods of time away, so it's nice to have homes in those places. I have one in Chicago, LA, New York and a cabin in the mountains. The cabin is for fun, not for work," he added with a laugh.

"And well, my mom's house in Hawaii. So, five if you count that."

I just shook my head in awe as I looked up at the building. I couldn't even imagine living a life like that.

"Welcome home, Mr. August," the doorman said as he opened the door for us.

I followed Kris through the lobby and into a private elevator that said "penthouse." *Of course, he lives in the penthouse.* The doors shut and the elevator started its climb.

"So, Mr. August," I said as I kissed his neck and trailed my hand down to his package. "Where are we going tonight?" I could feel him harden at my touch.

"To bed, if you keep that up," he said.

"Mmm. I like that idea."

"Trust me, I like that idea too. You and me in bed all day long. No clothes, no distractions." He kissed me, and the elevator stopped and opened. "But, I think you'll like what I have planned better."

My jaw dropped. This was not at all what I'd expected. The penthouse was beautifully decorated in a modern, but comfortable style with floor to ceiling windows that gave way to the most breathtaking views. The walls were lined with his gold and platinum records and pictures of him with what appeared to be every celebrity that was anyone in Hollywood.

I could hear yelling coming from another room. We turned the corner and entered what looked like a living room, but there were several racks of gowns and a few girls running around rearranging the dresses.

One older woman was barking orders at the younger ones. She paused when she saw us and ran her hands down her skirt as if she was removing wrinkles. "Mr. August and Ms. Johnson! Welcome home. Ms. Johnson, we need to get started. We don't have much time." She turned around and yelled, "Natalie, bring me the first dress!"

I was instantly overwhelmed and very confused.

Natalie pulled a full-length, bright blue dress covered in sequins off the rack. "Black. I told you she liked black," Kris told the crew, sending poor Natalie back to the dress rack.

"You have hair and makeup next," he told me before he kissed my forehead.

"Hair and makeup? Kris this is insane. Isn't this a little much for a night out?" I questioned.

"Generally, yes, but you're going to be my date to the Emmy's tonight, and I may have received a nomination."

"What?! Kris that is so amazing. I'm honored to be your date tonight. How did I not know that?" I felt horrible.

He laughed. "Well, I'm guessing you've been pretty distracted lately."

Yeah, distracted and sucking at my job apparently. Seriously Amber! I forced a smile. "You might have something to do with that." I laughed.

"The black one!" I heard the older woman yell.

I looked at Kris and raised my eyebrows. "Should I be afraid?" I joked.

"You're in good hands here. Only the best for my woman." He smiled. "Oh! And the bathroom is stocked with everything you should need but if anything's missing let me know and I'll get it for you."

"You had the bathroom stocked for me too? Wow, you thought of everything. You're truly amazing." I paused. "Oh and I get to shower in a real shower. Can I just go do that now? You can pick my dress." After showering in the green room showers for the past few weeks, a real shower sounded amazing.

"You pick your dress, and then you can shower before you get your hair done." Kris laughed. "Oh, and there might be a few things in the closest for you as well." He winked.

"Kris! I don't need all that."

"You haven't even seen it yet, and I just wanted you to feel comfortable here. It makes me happy to do things for you so just... Just don't be mad."

"I don't think I could be mad at you right now if I tried. Thank you for being so thoughtful." I place my hands on his stubbly cheek. "You know, I really like this unshaven look on you."

"Oh yeah? You think I should keep it?"

"Mmm. Yeah, I think it's sexy," I said as I came in for a kiss.

"Ms. Johnson." The older lady was trying to get my attention. "We really are running short on time."

Ugh. Cockblocker!

"You need to go pick a dress and get ready. I'm going to get myself ready, and I'll see you soon." He kissed me before leaving me alone with these crazy women in a room full of dresses.

"Ladies, let's make this quick. I have a hot shower waiting for me!" *And an even hotter man!* "I'm going to make this easy. Can I just save you some time and look through the dresses myself and pick one out?" I don't even know why I asked because I wasn't going to take no for an answer. I walked over to the rack of dresses and started sorting through them.

"Ms. Johnson, that is unconventional! It is our job to assist in dressing you," the older women shrewdly said.

"Well I don't think I need help dressing; I've been doing it myself my whole life. Thank you for your time, but this one right here will do. Where do I go next?" I asked as I pulled out a simple, yet elegant full-length, black gown that had the most beautiful lace design.

"Ma'am, right this way to the dressing room," Natalie said as she grabbed a box and a pair of black heels and led me to a bedroom that had a huge mirror set up and another group of people which looked like hair and makeup.

"Here are the undergarments for this dress and the shoes

that match," Natalie said as she set the box on the bed and placed the shoes on the floor. She took the dress from my hands. "I will hang this up here," she said as she placed the dress on a rack next to the mirror. "When you're ready, I will come back in and make sure it all works for you. Is that okay?"

"Yes, thank you. I appreciate your flexibility. I'm just not one for all that fuss." I smiled at her. "I'm going to go take a shower first if that's all right... Before all this takes place." I laughed and waved my arms around at all the chaos I was surrounded by.

"No worries, Ms. Johnson, I understand. The bathroom is right through those doors," she pointed at a set of double doors across the room.

"Thank you, Natalie. And you can just call me Amber."

"Yes, Ms. John... I mean, Amber," she said as she walked over to the hair and makeup crew to fill them in.

I opened the double doors and the largest bathroom I had ever seen sprawled out before me. It was covered in gray marble tile with a white claw-foot tub in the middle of the room. Off to the left, there was a glass shower big enough for at least ten people, and to the right was a luxurious couch.

Straight ahead was a double vanity stocked with all my favorite things. *Seriously how does he do that?* I didn't know if I should be impressed or creeped out that he knew so much about me already. Right now, I didn't care. I just wanted in that shower.

I stripped off my clothes and tossed them on the couch, then took the most amazing shower of my life. I just stood there for what seemed like an hour and let the water run over me. It was the first time in a while that I could just catch my breath and let this all sink in.

In only a matter of weeks, my life had changed so dramatically. I was completely content with my life before, but that was because I didn't know any different. I never knew what it felt like to be treated so well by a man. How it felt to be loved by a man and to have a man accept my love for him.

It was all so perfect; too perfect. I was almost afraid that it was too good to be true, and maybe it was. I had let my guard down which meant he had the power to totally destroy me. I shuddered at the thought, but it was a real possibility. Being with Kris was a risk. But all good things took sacrifice and risk, right?

I emerged from the bathroom in the white, fluffy robe that was left for me on the hook and was immediately swarmed by the hair and makeup ladies.

They sat me in the chair and went to town. They asked me my preferences, but in all honesty, I didn't care. I told them to do what they felt would look best.

All this fuss was too much for me. I was so excited that Kris had been nominated and I felt honored that I would get to be by his side, but otherwise, something like this wouldn't be for me. I was not about glitz, glamour, brand names and status. I would have been just as happy staying at home, eating pizza and watching a movie as long as Kris was by my side.

These ladies were bru—tal! I had two pulling on my hair and another one practically poking my eye out as she applied my makeup. She kept telling me to stop blinking. Easier said than done when you had a sharp object coming straight at your eyeball! A frenzy of activity swirled around me. I was sure the look on my face showed how annoyed I was.

"Ms. Johnson, can I get you something to drink?" someone asked. I was not even sure who at this point.

"God. Yes, please!" I very enthusiastically responded. "Anything with alcohol, please." She returned a few minutes later with a glass of champagne. "Thank you," I told her before quickly downing the glass and placing it on the table beside me, empty. Everyone paused momentarily as if in shock at how quickly I drank it, but I didn't care. It took the edge off. My nerves were starting to get the best of me. Soon I would be on the red carpet with Kris for all the world to see.

Deep breaths, Amber, you can do this!

My torture session ended, and Natalie returned to help get me dressed. I was a little nervous about this dress. I always had a hard time finding things that fit me right. I had a very curvy figure, so clothes were my enemy. This was the moment of truth. Natalie helped me slide the gown over the black, lacy undergarments and she zipped up the back. I sighed in relief when it zipped all the way. It was a tight fit.

I stepped into the heels and turned around to look at myself in the mirror for the first time. I just stood there, looking in the mirror, stunned. The dress was gorgeous. It was strapless and hugged my breasts perfectly. It fit all my curves perfectly. I turned from side to side, looking at myself from every angle. It had a pretty dramatic slit up the left side, which was a little more than I was comfortable with, but it worked.

"Absolutely stunning." I heard Kris say from behind me. I turned around and smiled at him as he entered the room. He looked unbelievably handsome in his tux. It fit his muscular frame like a glove, and he left the sexy stubble of facial hair that I loved. I could feel a fire ignite in my soul. *Damn this man!*

"There is just one thing missing," he said as he brushed my hair back and laid the black and white diamond necklace he had surprised me with on my neck. He trailed his touch with soft kisses. "You're the most beautiful woman I have ever seen," he whispered in my ear.

"You're the sexiest man I have ever seen," I said as I ran my hands down the front of his tux, wishing I could rip it off him.

"If you keep that up, we won't be making it out of the house." He smirked as he took my hand and fastened the matching bracelet around my tattooed wrist and kissed it. "I'll let you put these in," he said as he handed me the box with the earrings to complete the set.

I turned to the mirror to put them in, and he gently placed his hands on my hips, and I could see him intensely staring at me in the mirror with that look like he was going to totally consume me. The heat between us was strong. His lips were so warm on my back as he kissed and teased my exposed skin.

His hands wandered and gently squeezed my ass. "Good God, woman," he growled. The way he looked at me made me feel like a goddess. Definitely a new feeling for me.

"Mr. August, we are ready to depart," Donnie said from the doorway.

"You ready?" Kris winked at me.

"Ready as I'm ever going to be." I laughed as I picked up my clutch. Kris took my hand, and we were on our way.

The limo pulled up to the theater, and I could hear massive chaos outside and see flashes from the cameras. My stomach knotted. I could feel my grip on Kris's hand tighten. Not only was this overwhelming, but in the back of my mind, I was worried about whatever this security threat was that Kris was so concerned about. We really hadn't had a chance to talk more about it, so of course, my mind was thinking the worst.

Donnie opened the door, Kris stepped out, and I followed, his hand never leaving mine. The cameras were blinding and even disorienting. I was trying to keep a smile on my face and not let my *"what the fuck"* face show through.

Kris stopped several times to do interviews, and each time I tried to escape, but Kris wouldn't let go of my hand. Of course, the most popular questions were about our relationship. I couldn't help but smile when I heard Kris respond, "She's the love of my life." And then he kissed me as the world watched and millions of girls' hearts broke.

We finally made it to our seats and Kris proudly introduced me to his friends and cast members. We made small talk and laughed. Kris still didn't let go of my hand and never left my side. He spoiled me with kisses and kind words. I felt like the most important woman in the room even though I was most likely the least important one there.

We were surrounded by Hollywood's greatest talent in television, and I was with Kris August, one of the most talented. I always knew Kris was famous, but I just saw him as a regular person. It didn't really hit me until today, seeing him in this environment, how talented and distinguished he was. Yes, I guess I may have been a little biased, but he had a very successful music career and acting career in television and movies. There were not too many performers out there that could say that. I was so unbelievably proud of him and just watched him in awe.

Kris had nothing growing up, but had a dream and busted his ass with hard work, sweat, and tears and made it happen. If that wasn't the sexiest thing ever, I didn't know what was.

The lights went dim, and the program started. Kris's crime drama was cleaning house. They received award after award. I had no idea Kris also wrote and directed many of the episodes. I was so focused on learning about his musical career, I failed to learn about this side of him.

I think he spent more time on stage than he did in his seat. Every time, we celebrated together and he kissed me before he headed up to the stage.

The big one he was waiting for was up next. He gripped my hand tightly with anticipation. From the outside, he looked pretty calm, but I could tell he was nervous. Something I had never seen from him before.

"Ladies and gentlemen, the winner for outstanding lead actor in a drama series is…" there was a long pause, "Kris August."

The crowd erupted as they all stood up and clapped. We

hugged, and he kissed me. I whispered to him, "I'm so proud of you. I love you so much."

"I love you more than you will ever know," he told me before he headed up on stage to collect his award.

The crowd settled as he made his way to the podium. "Who knew a poor kid from the streets, who has made many poor choices in life could turn it all around and make their dreams come true?" The crowd laughed with him. "Wow! I'm so overwhelmed tonight. This means so much to me."

I could see tears in his eyes that he was fighting back and I could hear the emotions in his voice when he talked. "There are so many people I want to thank, including everyone I work with on the show. The cast and crew are all amazing, and I couldn't do it without you all. I need to thank my mother who always believed in me and sacrificed everything to make me the man I am today. And I want to say to every dreamer out there watching to never give up on your dreams. Work hard, and good things will come to you. I'm living proof of that! Amber, I love you, Baby! I can't wait to celebrate! Thank you!"

He blew me a kiss as he made his way off stage. The crowd clapped, and I had happy tears streaming down my face.

I swear every day I fell more in love with that man. My heart felt so full at that moment it could burst.

THE AFTER-PARTIES WERE FUN BUT SEEMED ENDLESS. I WAS exhausted and honestly ready to get Kris home to have our own celebration.

I was so relieved when the limo arrived back at the penthouse. Donnie told us to stay put for a minute while he checked the penthouse.

"I can't wait to get these heels and this dress off." I fidgeted.

"I can't wait to get that dress off you too. That's all I've been able to think about," Kris said. "Let me help." He reached down and slipped my heels off. His hand slowly trailing up my leg to my garter and his knuckles brushed against my clit, purposely teasing me, making me squirm with desire.

"Let's start by taking these off," he whispered as he pulled my panties off and put them in his pocket.

Donnie knocked on the door. "All clear, Mr. August."

Kris grinned at me with that devilish smile as he opened the door. "You coming?"

"Not yet, but I hope to be soon," I joked as I slid over him, teasing his already hard cock on my way out.

"That can be arranged," he said, playfully smacking my ass as I got out of the limo.

"Damn your ass looks so fucking good in that dress." Kris followed me into the elevator. As soon as the doors shut it was like he couldn't keep himself composed any longer. His hands groping my ass, his mouth claiming mine. I could feel his erection pressed against my mound as he tore into me like a teenager on prom night. I dropped my shoes as he unzipped my dress and shimmied it off me and I kicked it to the side.

The feeling of the elevator wall on my back was cold against my bare skin, but his touch was warm and drove me insane with need for him.

I frantically undid his pants as his fingers teased my wet entrance. The elevator arrived at the penthouse and the doors opened, but Kris didn't notice. His face was buried in my chest, nibbling and kissing all of me. I felt my knees weaken and my body tremble with desire for him. I begged him to take me.

"Is this what you want?" he groaned as his thick cock entered me, stretching me with every thrust.

"Yes," I moaned as he picked me up, diving deeper inside me. He carried me out of the elevator and navigated his way through the penthouse and into the bedroom. He laid me on the bed, still buried deep inside me.

The fluffy, gray down blanket was soft and smelled like Kris's cologne. I was engulfed in his scent. His big, muscular body hovered over me, surrounded me, making me feel safe, secure and loved. We took our time, exploring and enjoying each other's bodies in a slow and sensual way like we had never done before. The sensation of his hands lovingly caressing my body, while he claimed every inch of me, had me breathless and begging for my release.

His lips tenderly nibbled my breasts as I trembled with pleasure beneath him. I never wanted him to stop. I wanted to freeze time and stay here like this forever with him.

I always thought intense feelings of love and pleasure were a myth, something found only in the movies, but it was so real, and now that I found it, I never wanted to give it up. He was my soul mate. My Dante. My love.

Tears began to roll from my eyes as waves of intense pleasure ripped through my body. I found my release in more ways than one. I was overcome with so many emotions all at once that pleasure, love and years of pent-up frustrations and despair poured out of me. It was as if the happiness that I'd found with Kris made me realize how much pain I was in before and it needed to come out so I could move on.

"Amber." Kris froze. "Are you okay? Why are you crying?" Kris asked as he wiped the tears from my face and kissed my cheek.

"Please don't stop. Kris, please," I pleaded. "They're happy tears. I promise."

I placed my hands on his stubbly cheeks and looked deep into his dark eyes. "I have never felt more alive in my life," I kissed him. "I love you so much. Please don't ever stop," I cried. I begged. I had never begged a man for anything in my life; I was too strong for that. But at that moment, I was completely vulnerable. I conceded, but not to weakness, to love. I needed him like I needed air to breathe.

"Baby, I love you more than you will ever know." He looked deep into my eyes. "I have waited for you my whole life, Amber." He kissed me deeply, our tongues mingling passionately.

The heat between us was undeniable, and the love was strong.

He made love to me until we fell asleep tightly wrapped in each other's arms as the moonlight softly lit the room.

I WOKE THE NEXT MORNING STILL WRAPPED IN HIS STRONG arms. His fingers were lightly trailing up and down my arm.

"Good morning, Beautiful," Kris said. His voice was rugged still from sleep.

"Good morning." I smiled as he kissed my forehead.

"We need to get going soon so I can get back for the show tonight."

"Ugh, I wish we could stay. This has been so nice." I pouted.

"I know. Just a few more weeks on the road and then we can have this all this time."

"But how is that even going to work? I only have another week left before I have to get back to the office." I sighed. "And you'll still be on tour."

"You could quit your job and stay with me," he said.

"I'm not going to quit my job, Kris."

"Why? You don't have to work. I can take care of you. I want to take care of you."

"I'm not quitting my job," I said flat out.

"Okay, then I'll quit my job," he joked.

"You're not going to quit your job. Stop playing." I laughed.

"I would, Amber. I would quit in a heartbeat if I had to choose between you and my career."

"Kris, I would never ask you to choose. I know how much you love your job."

"True, but I finally found something I love more." He smiled. "You!"

I kissed him, and he pulled me on top of him. He was rock hard and ready. *I swear this man must have a hard-on 24/7.*

His phone rang, but he ignored it.

It rang again a few seconds later.

"You better get that," I said.

He snarled and swiped it off the nightstand. "It's security. I have to take this."

"It's fine. I'm going to take advantage of that amazing shower again before we leave," I said as I gave him one more quick kiss before making my way to the bathroom.

A few minutes later, Kris entered the bathroom. He was naked and still sporting that beautiful hard-on. His body was chiseled perfection, and I couldn't help but stare.

"Amber," he said trying to get my attention.

"Yeah?"

"Did you hear me?" He laughed as he picked up his toothbrush and coated it with toothpaste.

"No. Did you say something?" I realized I wasn't even moving, I was just standing there, intensely staring at him. I forced myself to at least to pretend to shower. "Must be the water. It's loud in here." *Good cover, Amber!* The truth was I was just totally lost in his body. *Mmm, his ass is just amazing.*

"Uh huh." He smirked. "I said, they found the person responsible for the threats. It was Lily."

"Lily?! As in your ex, Lily?"

He sighed. "Yeah, that would be her. But they detained her, so the security threat is over. She won't be bothering us again," he mumbled out as he brushed his teeth.

"That's good. Where was she?" I asked as I lathered my hair in shampoo, relieved.

"Apparently she had been following us around for a while. They found her in the parking garage early this morning, sleeping." He rinsed his mouth out and headed toward the shower.

"Following us? That's...creepy." I shivered at the thought of her following us around, and God knew for how long or what she saw. *Shit!* I wondered if she was the girl that I had been seeing around everywhere. Thankfully, they'd found her.

"You don't have to worry about it anymore. She isn't well. I'm making sure she gets the help she needs."

Isn't well? I wonder that means. He's said that a few times about her.

He stepped into the shower. My mind quickly forgot everything else except for this sexy beast of a man in front of me. He grabbed some soap and lathered himself up; teasing and taunting me with every movement. I realized I had stopped moving again and I may have even been drooling a little.

"See something you like, Ms. Johnson," he teased.

I couldn't even respond. I let out the most uncomfortable giggle ever. *Oh, that was sexy, Amber!*

He took the soap and squeezed some over my body. It was cold as it trailed down my breasts and onto my stomach. I felt my body respond with goosebumps, but his hands quickly warmed me as he lathered me up.

"I think we need to finish what we started before the phone interrupted us."

Best idea ever!

WE ARRIVED BACK AT THE ARENA JUST IN TIME FOR KRIS TO GET

to his pre-show meet and greets, and I headed to the bus to unpack and catch up on some work.

I hated missing the show, but I had promised Rebecca an insider story from the awards, and it was due soon, so I needed some quiet time to work. It was hard to stay focused because I was distracted by reading all the stories online and looking at all the pictures of Kris and me from last night.

I was also curious about the situation with Lily and was trying to see if there was anything online, but there wasn't, not even one picture.

I just found this whole thing weird. How was there already so many pictures of Kris and me out there and stories all over, but nothing, not one piece of information on them?

I contemplated having my research assistant do some digging for me, but I just didn't feel right going behind Kris's back. Plus, I hadn't even really pressed him for the details. I needed to give him the chance to fill me in first. I just needed to make it a priority to ask. Talking wasn't something we did often.

Ugh! Focus, Amber!

I looked at the time. Kris should be done soon, and I needed to get this story submitted so I could meet him after the show. I wanted to be there when he was done, plus I hadn't talked to Jen in a while and I was hoping to see her so we could catch up.

I quickly gave my story another look. I made a few edits, attached a few photos and hit send. I still felt like I was selling myself out with these stories, but I guess as long as it was major events and not our daily lives I was okay with it.

I grabbed my VIP pass, threw it around my neck and headed down the stairs of the bus. A cool breeze hit me as I opened the door and stepped out. There was a chill in the dark air, and it was eerily quiet. I could vaguely hear the music coming from the arena in the distance, but that was it.

The buses were parked in a secluded area where the fans couldn't see them, so there weren't even any groupies hanging around. It felt...off. I could feel the hair on my arms go up and I shivered. I walked a little faster. I just wanted to get inside.

"Amber!" I heard someone from behind me yell. I turned around. It was Jen.

"Hey!" I was so happy to see her...or anyone for that matter. "I was hoping I was going to see you tonight," I said as I leaned in to give her a hug.

"Yeah, sorry I've just been busy," she coldly said as she quickly backed away from me. "Maybe we can go back to your bus and...catch up?"

"Well, I was going to meet Kris after the show, but that's fine. I feel like I haven't seen you in a while." I pulled out my phone. "I'll just text him and let him know." We started walking back to Kris's bus. There was an awkward silence between us.

I hope I didn't do something to upset her.

I opened the bus door and motioned for Jen to head in. My phone vibrated, so I paused. It was Kris letting me know he just finished and would meet me at the bus when he could get away. I smiled and headed up the stairs to meet Jen.

"Everything okay?" I asked as I got to the top of the stairs. I froze, and my phone fell out of my hands, making a loud thump on the floor. Jen was standing there with a gun pointed at me. Her face was completely void of any emotion.

My heart was pounding so hard I thought it was going to break through my chest. *Run Amber!* I slowly turned my head to see how far the door was.

"Don't even think about moving!" she yelled at me as if she knew what I was thinking.

"Jen, I...I don't understand." My voice was shaking, and I could barely get the words out.

"I warned you to stay away from him, but you didn't

listen," she snarled at me.

"Kris? This is about Kris? I don't...I don't--"

"Shut up!" she screamed.

I jumped. A tear rolled down my cheek. I could hear my phone vibrating on the floor nearby.

"It was supposed to be me! Then you came along and stole him from me. I became invisible as soon as you arrived. I was nothing more than his errand girl."

I could see her hands trembling as she kept the gun pointed at me. "Jen, I didn't know. I didn't know you two were a thing. I would have never..." I shook my head. "I'm sorry. I--"

"We weren't a thing. We never got a chance to be 'a thing' because you arrived," she interrupted me. "You ruined everything!" Her words were sharp.

I could hear people outside. I knew it was only a matter of time before Kris arrived.

"I worked so hard to get here. To get my chance with him, but you...*you*!" She shook the gun at me. "You have to die."

She looked around and spotted the box with my jewelry from last night on the table. "I'll make it look like a robbery. No one will suspect it was me." She smirked and tilted her head. "When you're gone, I'll be there to comfort Kris."

She lifted the gun to aim.

My heart sank. Tears rolled down my face as I pleaded for my life. I closed my eyes. I heard the deafening sound of the gun go off and someone knocked me to the ground. I could feel my blood pouring down my arm, but I didn't feel any pain.

I heard Jen scream...or was it me?

I was so disoriented. My ears were ringing, my vision was blurry, adrenaline pumping through my heart at a speed I had never felt before. I could feel the weight of someone on top of me.

The gun went off again. I jumped. Every bone in my body rattled.

I froze waiting for something else to happen, but there was nothing. Total silence.

It all happened so fast, a matter of seconds. The longest seconds of my life. I could see I was in a pool of blood. I needed to get help. I shook the person on top of me, but nothing. I rolled them off me.

God, no! Please, no!

I screamed, "*No! Kris!* Kris, wake up." I shook him, but he was lifeless. "Help!" I screamed as loud as I could, over and over.

Jen laid lifeless just a few inches away in a pool of her own blood. She had taken her own life, and now I saw why. I wasn't shot, it was Kris.

I tried to find where he was shot, but there was just so much blood. "Kris, please don't leave me," I pleaded. I cried. "I love you so much. Don't you leave me."

I was frantically searching for the bullet wound. "Someone! Help!" I yelled as he laid there, lifeless in my arms.

A storm of security finally came rushing in. It felt like a lifetime, but it was only seconds.

"Help him!" I screamed as they rushed around us.

"Ms. Johnson, are you hurt? Ms. Johnson, we need you to tell us what happened."

"Save him! God, please save him!" I yelled as I pushed their hands away from me. "He's dying!"

I was frantic. Why weren't we moving? Why weren't we on the way to the hospital?

There was a frenzy of activity around me. I could hear the sirens near. Tears flowing from my eyes, blurring my vision. I could see the flashing red lights out the window as a group of men quickly surrounded Kris and carried him out, leaving me screaming in a pool of his blood.

PART THREE

I COULD HEAR THE STEADY of beeping and mumbled speaking in the distance as I tried to open my eyes. My head ached. I slowly came to. I was confused. Where was I? What happened?

Kris!

I shot up in the bed. "Kris!" I called out to him. I looked around, but I was in a hospital room alone. I could see there was a crowd of police officers outside my room. A nurse rushed through the door.

"Ms. Johnson, it's good to see you awake. I'm Nancy, your nurse. How are you feeling?"

I started pulling all the cords off me. I needed to find Kris.

"Ms. Johnson, we need you to stay in bed. You've had quite the trauma, and we had to sedate you."

Trauma! You can fucking say that again! "I'm fine. I need to see Kris. Where is he?" I asked as I tried to get out of bed, but my legs wouldn't hold me. *What the fuck?*

"Ms. Johnson, Kris is still in surgery. You can't see him right now. You need to worry about your own recovery right now. I need you to get back in bed."

"Kris is alive?" Tears rolled down my face. I was relieved, terrified, and confused. "My own recovery? I'm fine. It was Kris that was hurt! I need to go to him. Why am I even in this bed?" I asked as I tried to pull the wires off of me again.

"Ms. Johnson, I need you to calm down. We'll explain to you what happened." She motioned to one of the officers to come in.

"You were shot in your arm, but you'll be fine." The officer joined her blocking my way so I couldn't leave. "As I mentioned, we had to sedate you, and you're on some pain meds that are going to make you a little woozy, so I need you to get back in bed."

"Shot? I wasn't shot. Kris was shot."

"Ms. Johnson, we think the bullet passed through Kris and went into your arm," the officer said.

I looked down at my arm, and it was covered in a blood-stained bandage. My head started to spin, and my body felt like it weighed a thousand pounds. My heart broke at the thought of Kris in surgery.

"He took the bullet for me, didn't he?" I broke down right there in that bed. Tears streaming uncontrollably down my cheeks. "This is all my fault."

"Ms. Johnson, we are not exactly sure what happened, but we would like to get a statement from you as soon as possible," the officer said.

"It was Jen. It was all Jen," I cried as I curled up in the bed shaking uncontrollably. I couldn't breathe, and the room was spinning around me.

"I think that's enough for now," I heard the nurse say before I passed out.

When I came to again, my body ached. It hurt to move. The sun was shining so bright through the window I had to squint my eyes to see. Shawn was sitting in a chair, and his head was resting on the bed near my hand. He looked like shit. I took my hand and gently ran it over his hair. He jumped up.

"You're awake," he said with a big smile on his face. "How are you feeling?"

"I'm fine," I said, but I could tell I had been heavily drugged. "How's Kris? Please tell me he's okay?"

"He's out of surgery, but he hasn't woken up yet. No one's been able to see him." He frowned.

Tears escaped my eyes again. I was relieved he was alive but worried that he wasn't awake yet. "He needs to be okay," I sobbed.

Shawn grabbed my hand to comfort me. "He's a fighter, Amber. He'll pull through. I know it."

"Where was he shot? How bad is he? Did the doctors tell you anything?"

"They said he took it in the upper chest and it exited out his shoulder. It didn't hit any major organs, but it got one of his arteries. They said they were able to repair the artery, but he lost a lot of blood." He rubbed his eyes. They were red, and it looked like he had been crying.

"Amber, what happened?"

"I…" I paused and tried to recall how it all happened, but the details were so fuzzy. "It all happened so fast, I'm not even really sure. I know I was headed into the arena to meet Kris, and Jen stopped me. She said she wanted to talk so we went back to the bus, and then she pulled a gun on me." I started to shiver.

"She wanted to kill me so she could be with Kris. I just remember she was about to shoot me and someone…" I took a deep breath. "Kris knocked me down. He saved me."

"Wait. Jen did this? To be with Kris? I don't understand." He stood up and started to pace the room. "Did they arrest her?"

"Shawn, she's dead. She killed herself. I…I don't understand either." I could feel my body start to shake uncontrollably and I found it hard to speak.

There was an awkward silence between us. The only sound was the beeping of the monitors as Shawn paced the room running his hands through his hair.

"Fuck!" he yelled causing me to jump. He stopped pacing, and his hands covered his face. "Jen and I…" He paused as if even saying her name hurt.

"Jen and you what, Shawn?" I questioned, but he didn't respond. "Oh Shawn, no!"

He dropped his hands and started to pace again. "It was new. I was lonely and she was easy to talk to. I really liked her. I just don't understand. I thought we had something. But apparently, she wanted Kris. And she was fucking crazy! And now she's dead. How did I not see this?" He finally sat back down in the chair.

"Shawn, I'm so sorry." I grabbed his hand. "I don't think anyone saw this coming." We just sat there together in silence for what seemed like an eternity. Two people, broken and betrayed by the same person, finding comfort in each other's company.

"Hey, Shawn," I finally said softly.

"Yeah?"

"I don't know where my phone is, and I really need to call my son. I don't know how much is on the news, but I don't want him to worry. Can I maybe use your phone to call him?"

"I already tracked him down last night to make sure I got to him before the news broke. Don't turn on the TV, it's everywhere, and there are reporters camped outside this place." He sighed. "I've been sending your son updates. He's understandably worried, but he's fine."

He handed me his phone. "I'm going to see if I can get an update on Kris. I'll give you some privacy."

"Thank you, Shawn. You're amazing."

He stopped at the door, "Oh, and the officers outside still want to talk to you. They seem pretty eager to get your statement. I had to fight to even get in here. I'm sure they will be in soon now that you're awake. I'll try to distract them to give you a few minutes." He dropped his head and left the room.

I quickly called my son. It was amazing to hear his voice. He wanted to fly out, but I made him promise to stay at school. I didn't want him to miss anything. Once he realized I was fine, I think he was okay with that but was eager for me to get back home and I honestly couldn't wait to see him. I missed him so much it hurt.

Shawn was right. The officers entered the room just as I was hanging up the phone. They questioned me for what seemed like hours. I had to tell them what happened over and over again. I was exhausted, and I just wanted to talk to Shawn to see how Kris was.

"Are we done yet, Officer? I really don't have anything else to share."

"We can be done for now. Please don't leave town without notifying us. We'll be in touch if we have any more questions." He closed his notebook and nodded at his partner signaling it was time to go.

"Yes, Officer. Thank you." I threw my head back on the pillow and closed my eyes. I needed sleep, but I was too anxious to hear about Kris.

I turned over and tried to find a comfortable position, but my body ached.

I noticed that I still had dry spots of blood stained on my skin. Kris's blood. I frantically started to rub it off. Tears exploded down my face, my heart racing as the memories of what happened came rushing back to me. It wasn't coming off. It looked like someone tried to clean me up, but they couldn't fully wash away the truth of that night.

The nurse walked in. "How are you feeling, Ms. Johnson?"

"Please help!" I was panicked. "I can't get it off." I continued to rub my skin raw.

"Ms. Johnson, I need you to relax. What can I help you with?"

"His blood. Please… I can't…" I was crying so hard I couldn't get the words out.

"Okay. Okay." She pulled the blanket I was using to clean my skin out of my hands. "We will get you cleaned up. Do you feel up to a shower?"

"Yes. Please," I pleaded.

She unhooked me from all my monitors and helped me out of bed. My legs were still weak, but I could at least stand, and I had the nurse to lean on. She helped me to the bathroom. Tears were still uncontrollably falling from my eyes; I couldn't stop crying. She undressed me and helped me into the shower.

I just stood there and watched the blood-tainted water run off my body and down the drain. I grabbed the soap and scrubbed my skin over and over again. I couldn't get clean enough. The blood quickly washed away, but it wasn't the blood I was trying to erase; it was that night. It was the memories of Kris bleeding out in my arms as I sat there helpless. Those memories were never going to wash away.

Shawn returned shortly after I got a fresh gown and returned to my bed. My heart broke for him.

"Hey," he forced a smile. "You look a little better." He handed me a bag. "Here I brought you some food."

"Thank you." I too forced a smile and placed the food on the tray that already had a full plate of hospital food that I couldn't stomach to eat.

"No more monitors. That's a good sign, huh? Does that mean you get to go home soon?"

"They said I'll be discharged in the morning."

I looked at Shawn. "I hate to ask, but could you maybe

bring me some clothes? Mine are, well…covered in blood and I don't have anything else except for this hospital gown."

"Of course. I'll make sure we have something here for you in the morning."

"Thank you. I'm sorry to be such a burden right now."

"Amber, you're not a burden. We're friends, and you're my best friend's girl. We're in this together."

"How are you…um, feeling?" I stumbled over my words. I was worried about him, and I didn't want to stir things back up for him.

"I'll be fine," he bluntly said. "You need to eat something," he insisted.

"I'm not hungry."

"Yeah, me neither," he said as he plopped down in the chair.

"Any updates?" I eagerly asked.

"Still not awake. The doctor seems optimistic that he'll wake up soon."

"When can I see him?"

"They're not letting anyone in that isn't family right now. His mom is flying in today and should be here soon. I'm hoping she'll be able to change that."

My heart sank. It killed me to not be able to be with him. "Fuck this." I whipped the blankets off and hopped out of bed. "Do you know where his room is?" I asked.

"Yes. But what are you doing?" He jumped up in front of me.

"I'm going to see him. Even if just for a minute. Can you take me there please?"

He stepped out of my way. "Do I have a choice?"

"Nope."

I followed Shawn to the intensive care unit to a room at the end of a hall. I looked around and didn't see anyone that would stop me. I took a deep breath and looked at Shawn one last time as if looking for permission even though I was going in without it.

I slid open the glass door and quickly closed it behind me. The curtain was drawn, blocking Kris from my view, but I could hear the machines beeping.

My heart was beating out of my chest. I was terrified of what I was going to see. I slowly walked toward the bed and peeked around the curtain.

Kris laid there with his beautiful dark eyes closed. His skin was pale, and his body lifeless. He didn't have a gown on; he was shirtless and had a bandage across his chest and shoulder. It pained me to see him like this.

"Baby, I'm so sorry," I whispered as I gently touched his lifeless hand. I just stood there watching him as if he was going to wake up any second, but he didn't.

I carefully laid down next to him on the side that wasn't bandaged and curled up close to him. His body was warm, and I could hear his heart beating. I rested my hand over his heart so I could feel it. It was the only real thing that told me he was alive.

"You need to wake up, Kris." I started to cry. "I didn't think I needed anyone in this world until I met you. You changed that. Now I can't imagine my life without you. I know it's silly, it's only been a few weeks, but you've changed me in a way I never thought possible. You taught me I'm capable of loving a man, and even more that I'm worthy of being loved."

I gently traced his tattoos on his chest with my fingers. "You can't leave me, Kris. I need more time with you," I cried. "You need to fight! You have so many people that love you."

Lying there next to him made me feel safe for the first time since this happened. I felt whole again. Time slowed as I rested there just listening to his heart.

"Amber," I heard Shawn whisper. "Amber, time to go."

"No!" I yelled as quietly as I could. "Not yet. I need more time."

"You have like thirty more seconds," Shawn said. I heard the sliding door close.

"I hate to leave you alone, but I have to go. I promise I'll be back." I kissed Kris on his cheek. "And you better be awake."

I crawled out of bed and stood there for a few more seconds, just hoping he would open his eyes, but he didn't.

"I love you, Kris," I said as I squeezed his hand before I walked out.

THE NEXT MORNING, I AWOKE FEELING HOPEFUL FOR THE DAY ahead of me. I was being discharged, and after seeing Kris yesterday, I just knew he would be okay; I felt it in my soul.

I showered and sat around watching the news as I waited for the doctor to officially give me the okay to leave.

The news was still heavily covering the story about Kris. Apparently, when they searched Jen's home in Atlanta, they found evidence that she had not only been obsessed with Kris but that she had been plotting for a long time on how to get close to him.

Every time they showed her picture, it made me shiver. Those are memories that will be with me for a lifetime.

"Hey, I thought I told you not to watch the news," Shawn said as he entered my room.

"I know. I tried not to, but it's on every channel." I frowned. "And I wanted to know what everyone was reporting." I hit the power button on the remote to turn it off.

"Any updates on Kris?" I asked.

"Well, his mom is here. She said it appeared he was trying to move his hands last night, but he still hasn't woken up yet."

"That's good, right?"

"Yeah, the doctor said that was a good sign."

"How are you doing? You don't look like you've slept." In fact, he was in the same clothes as yesterday.

"I'm better today. Thank you." He faked a smile. "Here, I brought you some stuff." He rolled my suitcase in. "I didn't think you would want to go back on the bus to get your things, so I had them all packed up for you. I even got your laptop and," he paused and dug something out of his pocket, "I was able to get your phone back." He handed it to me.

"Shawn, you're amazing." I hugged him. "Thank you! I just assumed I was never getting my things back."

"Well, you almost didn't. But the police gathered everything they needed, and it's a closed case, so they were able to let me on the bus, which is why I'm a little late."

"I'm so sorry you had to see that, Shawn."

"It's okay. I needed to. I think it gave me some closure."

He sat down. "How could I have been so blind? How didn't I see what she was?"

"You're a good guy, and sometimes our emotions toward people can blind us." I sat on the bed across from him. "And no one saw it. I shared a bus with her and hung out with her and didn't see it. I mean, I guess when I look back, she was constantly trying to tell me what a bad guy Kris was so I wouldn't hang out with him." I stopped and tried to think back. "I guess I see that as a warning now, but then, how would I have known? How would you have known?"

"Yeah, I guess you're right."

There was a knock on the door, and I heard it open.

"Ms. Johnson?" The nurse walked in. "I have your discharge instructions. Is now a good time to go over them with you?"

"That's my cue to head out," Shawn said. "When you're done, we're all in the intensive care waiting room." He waved as he walked out.

The nurse was quick and to the point. She provided me with a prescription for the pain, along with another one for an antibiotic, and told me to call if I was having problems with the stress.

I was anxious to get over to the waiting room, so I quickly got dressed, gathered my belongings and headed over to wait with Shawn, my suitcase in tow. I really didn't know where I was going to go; I had no place to go. I guess my plan was to just camp out in the waiting room until Kris got better and then go from there.

I found the waiting room, and it was packed full of people. I saw Shawn and a few others I recognized staked out in the corner of the room. "Hey, do you mind if I join you?" I asked.

"Of course not. Have a seat." Shawn patted the open chair next to him.

"Are Jason and Brad here?" I looked around but didn't see them.

"They were here earlier, but went to the hotel to get some sleep."

"Have you slept?" I questioned Shawn again. "Because it certainly doesn't look like it."

"I got a few hours."

Liar!

"So what hotel are you staying at?" I asked

"Well…I…I didn't actually go to the hotel yet. I slept here." He put his head in his hands. "He's my best friend. I just can't leave him."

"I know." I put my hand on his back. "I don't think I can leave either." There was a long silence between us. "So, any updates?"

"Nothing new. His mom has been back there with him and giving us updates every so often."

The thought of meeting his mom made my stomach knot. She sounded like an amazing woman, but I would have loved to have met her under different circumstances. *I wonder if she even knows who I am?*

Waiting was grueling. We didn't talk much. We all just sat there. The television was on in the room, but I didn't think anyone was watching it. Every now and then we would get up and take a quick walk to stretch our legs or use the bathroom, but that was it. It felt like time slowed. It felt like an entirety.

I tried to write a little, but my mind was distracted, and I couldn't focus. I turned to Facebook, but I had a few hundred notifications, and I was immediately overwhelmed and wasn't ready to see what people were saying about what happened yet.

I tried to tackle my emails, but I read one from Rebecca, who, of course, wanted my inside story yet again on what happened. Something I was not willing to even think about.

I texted Julie a few times. She had offered to fly out to be with me, but I insisted she stay home and that I would see her soon.

I wanted so badly to find something to take my mind off of the waiting, but my mind wouldn't let me do anything except sit there and worry.

My eyelids were becoming heavier by the minute, but I couldn't even sleep. It felt like I had been sitting in that chair for days, but in reality, it had only been a few hours.

I decided I needed to get up and take a walk to get some blood flowing. I did a few laps around the floor and explored a few hallways. I didn't want to go far; I was afraid I would miss something if I were gone for too long.

It felt good to walk, though, and it helped clear my mind of all the negative thoughts. I was thinking back to the last night Kris and I had together at his place and how amazing it felt to be in his arms. Just the memory of it brought a smile to my face.

I missed that feeling so much, and I couldn't wait until he

was better so we could pick up where we left off. I missed out on forty years with him, and I didn't want to waste any more time. I felt so strongly that he was my soul mate. I know I fought it at first, but once I let my guard down, I'd known there was something special about him. He was the love of my life, my soul mate, and the short amount of time we had together just wasn't enough.

I decided it was time to head back, but I quickly realized I was so lost in my own thoughts that I had no idea where I was or how to get back. Every hall I turned down looked the same, and I couldn't find any signs or anything to get me back to where I needed to be.

No worries, I will text Shawn. I reached into my pocket for my phone and realized I didn't bring it with me. *Fucking brilliant, Amber!*

I just kept walking, knowing eventually I would see a sign or find someone that could tell me where to go, but I felt like I was going in circles and I had been gone too long and was starting to panic.

"Ma'am. Are you okay?" a tall doctor wearing scrubs asked as he walked toward me.

"No, I'm apparently lost. I'm trying to find my way back to the intensive care waiting room. Can you maybe tell me how to get back there? I don't know how I got so turned around." I ran my hand through my hair to get it out of my face. It was damp, and I realized I must have been sweating. I'm sure I looked like a hot mess.

"I'm actually headed that way. I can take you." He turned the opposite direction I was going and motioned for me to follow him.

"Wow, so I wasn't even going in the right direction?"

"No." He chuckled. "It's okay. It's a big hospital, and it's easy to get turned around."

"Yeah, apparently." I let out a nervous laugh. There was an

awkward silence as I followed him for what seemed like several minutes.

"Just right down this hall and the door to the waiting room is on your left." He pointed.

"Thank you, I really appreciate it," I said as I hurried back.

"Amber, where have you been?" Shawn asked.

"I just needed to go for a walk, and then I got lost and I didn't have my phone and this nice doc--"

"Amber! He's awake!" Shawn excitedly yelled at me.

"What? You mean... He... While I was... Oh my God! He's awake? Is he okay? What do you know? Tell me. When can I see him?" My heart was racing.

"You just missed his mom. She wanted to get back to him, so she just gave a quick update. He's awake, and the doctors are in with him now checking him out. She said he seemed a little confused, but he was able to talk."

"That's great news! When can I see him? Did she say?"

"She... Well..." He rubbed the back of his neck like he was uncomfortable.

"What? What is it?"

"He said your name when he woke up like he was looking for you. His mom said she told him she would bring you to him."

I sighed. "And I wasn't here!"

"No. Well, yes, she was hoping to see you. But..." He stopped and looked away. "He said no."

"He said no? Said no to what?"

"To seeing you." Shawn paused and then quickly added, "Amber, he was confused. He doesn't want to see anyone. I'm sure he wants to see you, and he just needs some time to pull himself together. He's a proud man, and I'm sure he just wants—"

"He doesn't want to see me?" I sat down. "He doesn't want to see me," I whispered it back to myself as if hearing it again would make it real. I felt a pit growing in my stomach. I wanted to vomit. I closed my eyes and rested my head in my hands.

"Amber." I felt Shawn sit down next to me. "He's been through a lot and just woke up. I'm sure once he's more alert he'll want to see you."

I couldn't even answer him. I just looked up and gave him a fake smile. Maybe he was right, or maybe Kris blamed me for what happened. Or maybe he wasn't really in love with me at all, and this was all just a game to him after all. The tour was obviously over, so I guess he was done with me too.

I was so relieved that Kris was awake and it sounded like he was going to be okay, but negative thoughts swirled around in my mind at a tremendously fast rate, until I finally let it sink in that I just needed to wait.

Maybe Shawn was right, and Kris just needed some time. Regardless, my heart was broken. I felt broken.

"We're all going to head to the hotel. You should come," Shawn said.

"Just like that, everyone's leaving?"

"Well, she told us we should all go get some rest, and I think she's right. He's awake, he's going to be fine, and we should give him some space. He doesn't want to see anyone right now. We'll be back tomorrow."

"You guys can go. I'm staying. I can't leave yet."

Shawn stood up. "Amber––"

I interrupted him. "Shawn. Thank you for helping take care of me, but I'm fine. I promise. I just really need to stay."

"Okay. Just call me if you need anything. I'll text you the hotel information in case you change your mind. I'll have a room waiting for you."

I stood up and gave him a hug. "Thank you. For everything."

"I'll be back in the morning," he said as he made his way out the door.

"AMBER?" I HEARD SOMEONE SAYING MY NAME, WAKING ME from a light sleep. I was curled up in the reclining chair in the waiting room. It was so uncomfortable, but I must have dozed off.

I cracked open my eyes. "Yes?" It was dark outside, and the clock on the wall said it was 1:00 am.

"You're Amber, right?" the beautiful older woman asked.

I sat up and rubbed my eyes. "Yes, I'm Amber."

"I'm Nalani. I'm Kris's mom."

"Oh my God. Yes. Hello! It's nice to finally meet you. Is he okay?" I stood up and tried to shake her hand, but instead, she embraced me in a hug.

"Yes. Yes, he's doing well. He's sleeping." she smiled. "I've heard so much about you. It is good to finally meet you. Please sit back down," she said as she sat in the chair next to mine. "I thought everyone went to the hotel?"

"Yeah, they left earlier. I... I just couldn't bring myself to leave yet. I'm sorry. I know Kris doesn't want to see anyone. I just couldn't leave."

"It's okay. I know he was worried about you too. He was very relieved to know you were okay." She took a sip of her coffee. "I can tell he loves you very much. I've never seen my boy in love before."

"But he still doesn't want to see me though, does he?"

"No. He still doesn't want to see anyone." She shook her head. "He's definitely not himself, Dear. We're going to be transporting him back home tomorrow. The doctors said he can travel and he wants to go home."

"To Chicago?" I asked.

"No, to Hawaii."

"Tomorrow? So soon?" That pit in my stomach was back again and this time with a vengeance. I wanted to cry, but I needed to be strong. I looked down at my tattoo as if it was going to magically make me stronger. It didn't work.

"Yes. I know it seems soon, but the doctors gave him the okay to leave as long as we provided him with the proper care, which of course we will. He'll need a little rehab to get back to normal, but the doctors think he will be back to his old self in no time."

"That's... That's great news." A tear escaped my eye despite trying to hold it back. "Sorry. I'm just so relieved to hear that he'll be okay," I said as I wiped the tear away.

"It's okay, Dear. I know I have had my share of tears over the past few days." She grabbed my hand. "He will be okay."

"I was just hoping to get to see him, but I'll respect his wishes." I hung my head in defeat. "I just don't know what to do now."

"Well, right now you need to get out of that chair and go to the hotel and get a good night's sleep in a proper bed. You need your rest too," she told me in a very motherly voice.

"I just don't want him to think I left him," I choked out as the tears began pouring from my eyes. The thought of leaving this hospital, leaving him, terrified me. What if I never saw him again? "What if he wakes and changes his mind?"

"You need your rest. I know he would agree. I will be sure to get a hold of you if anything changes."

"Can you..." I took a deep breath and pulled myself together. "Can you tell him I love him and I'll be there for him when he's ready? If that's what he wants." I wiped a few more tears away, then reached in my bag, pulled out some paper and a pen, wrote down my number and gave it to her. I wrote another note to Kris that simply said, *I'm sorry. I love you. -A.*

"Can you make sure he gets this?"

"Of course," she said as we stood up. She gave me a hug.

"Amber, I know he loves you very much. Just give him some time."

"Thank you. It was nice to meet you. I wish it were under better circumstances." I tried to smile, but I don't think it was very convincing. I felt lost, and it was like at that moment I went numb. I didn't want to feel anything anymore. It was all too much. I watched her leave and head down the hallway back to Kris.

I thought about texting Shawn, but it was late, and I didn't want to bother him. He had sent me the address and told me a key would be at the front desk waiting for me, so there really wasn't any need to bother him. I requested an Uber, grabbed my things and defeatedly left the hospital alone.

The Uber arrived quickly, and it was just a short ride to the hotel. The key was at the desk like promised, and I made my way to my room. My body was trembling uncontrollably. The door shut behind me and I slid to the floor. The room was spinning, and I couldn't breathe. The pain in my chest was real; my heart was broken.

I grabbed my knees; I needed to hold on to something, anything. Tears sprung uncontrollably as I struggled to catch my breath.

Nalani's words kept echoing in my head on repeat, "*I know he loves you very much.*" But deep inside, I knew I wouldn't hear from him tomorrow, and I honestly didn't know if I ever would again.

I then became angry at myself for ever letting myself fall for him. I should have known better. I was better off alone.

I crawled over to the bed, climbed in and cried myself asleep.

IT'S DARK AND COLD OUTSIDE AND EERILY QUIET. I SEE A MAN

walking in my direction in the distance. I strain to see his face, but I can't quite make it out. I shiver as the cold air violates my skin. I keep walking toward the man.

"Who's there?" I yell at him.

"Amber?" he replies.

His face finally comes into focus. "Kris!"

I run to him, but right before I reach him, I hear a loud noise that causes me to freeze and cover my ears.

I stand there in shock as I watch Kris fall to the ground.

I sat up in bed, gasping for air and covered in sweat. My heart was beating out of my chest, tears falling. Every night it was the same nightmare. It had been a week since Kris left the hospital and flew to Hawaii with his mom. I flew home the same day. There really was no reason for me to stay. I didn't even tell Shawn I was leaving; I was too much of a mess to talk to anyone.

It had been a week, and I haven't heard from Kris or his mom. I swallowed my pride one night and sent him a text, just to let him know I was thinking of him and, nothing. No response. For all I knew, he didn't even have his phone, or maybe he changed his number.

My loneliness certainly wasn't welcome, but I took comfort in its familiarity. Today was the day I was going to join the world again. I planned to go back to work, and I was going to try to get back to some sort of normalcy. *Whatever that meant.*

I had the morning news on while I was getting ready for work, something I had been trying to avoid. They were still heavily covering the story, and while I didn't really want to re-live that night, it was the only way to learn about how Kris was doing.

My heart was broken, and I didn't understand why he wouldn't talk to me, but I still loved him and needed to know what was going on.

Every day I found myself disappointed when it was the same old news and nothing new. His publicist just kept providing general statements that he was doing well and working on recovery so he could get back to work, but nothing of substance and certainly no pictures or videos yet.

I turned the television off, threw the remote on the bed and headed to work; dreading what was lying ahead of me.

My commute was the same as it had always been, including seeing Dave's girlfriend, a constant reminder of my failed marriage and inadequacies.

It was at that moment that something just clicked in me. *Why do I put myself through this torture every day if I hate it?* Things needed to change, starting with getting out of this neighborhood. I mean, why did I need a big house when it was just me? I had always wanted to live in the city, closer to work maybe? There was nothing and no one here to stop me. I could do whatever I wanted. I didn't realize before how unhappy I was because I didn't know any differently, but now I knew what happiness was and this wasn't it. *Time to change that.*

I pulled into my usual parking space, picked up my phone and started a to-do list. First thing on the list: *Put the house on the market.*

I arrived at my desk and, again, it was the same as it had always been; nothing had changed, yet it felt different being there. It was quiet in the office, which I was thankful for. Rebecca and Julie were both at a conference and wouldn't be back for a few days so I knew they wouldn't be bothering me, and I really wasn't interested in making small talk with anyone today. I just wanted to get my day over with and get back to bed.

I sat down and was ready to just get to work and get through my day. I put in my earbuds, which was my usual ritual when I needed to get some serious writing done. I wanted to get this story finished as soon as possible, so I could just move on with my life.

I tried a few times over the past week to write, but it was all too painful thinking back on the memories of my time on tour and my time with Kris. The only motivation I had was hoping that Kris would read my words. Words that would tell the story of us. My story was going to be more than just what I originally set out to write. It needed to be bigger; he needed to be reminded.

It was 3:00 p.m. before I realized it. I was so deep into my story that I'd skipped lunch and hadn't moved all day.

It's not like I was eating much these days, but I was dying of thirst and needed some water. I walked with my head down, hoping I wouldn't have to talk to anyone, but of course, that didn't work. Person after person had to stop and give me a fake hug as if they really cared about me, which I knew they didn't. I was asked over and over again, "How are you doing?" And I would respond with the socially correct answer of, "I'm fine." I really wasn't fine, but I refused to let anyone know that. My pain was mine and mine alone. I wasn't one to let people in, except for Kris. How he broke down my wall, I still didn't know.

THE NEXT COUPLE OF DAYS WERE MORE OF THE SAME. WORK, avoid as many people as possible and then go home to bed. I was making serious progress on my story, and it actually started to feel good to write about it. It was therapeutic. I had so much in me, I could have written a book.

Yes, I should write a book! It was something I had always wanted to do, but just never made time to achieve. Another item added to my to-do list.

Later that evening, I was home just getting ready to crawl

into bed when my doorbell rang. *Ugh, seriously!* I reluctantly stomped to the door. I really wasn't in the mood to talk to anyone nor did I know who it could possibly be. I flung open the door only to find Dave standing there.

"What, Dave?" I questioned. Definitely not in the mood to deal with him.

"Wow, you look like shit, Amber." He looked me up and down with a scowl on his face.

"What do you want?"

"What's with the for-sale sign in the yard?"

"Well, Dave, that generally means someone is selling their house." I rolled my eyes at him.

"Why are you selling the house? You can't sell our house."

I laughed. "Our house? It's my house, Dave, and I can do what I want with it, and I don't have to tell you why." I started to shut the door, but he put his foot in the way. "Seriously, Dave, this isn't the time."

"You think now that you have some famous boy toy that you're big stuff now, don't you?"

"Fuck you, Dave!" I yelled as I noticed a black SUV parked across the street. There was a man in it with a camera. Obviously, paparazzi trying to get a story. They weren't getting anything from Kris so now they had found me. *Fucking fabulous. Just what I needed.*

"Dave, you see that truck parked out there? He has a camera and is capturing all of this, so I suggest you just fucking leave now before this gets ugly." Dave turned around to look, and I slammed the door and locked it.

I started to walk back to my room, and the doorbell rang again.

"Seriously, Dave!" I screamed as I stormed back to the door.

"Amber! It's me. Open up!"

"Julie?" I peeked out the window to make sure it was really

her. I opened the door and she about knocked me over with a hug.

"Girl! I have missed you so much. We have so much to catch up on, and I brought wine!" She handed me the bottle and made herself at home in the living room. "Get some glasses for that. Hey, so why is there a for-sale sign in your yard?" she asked without even missing a beat.

I set the glasses down. "Just time for a change, I guess."

"So where are you moving to?"

"I don't know yet. I just know I don't want to live here anymore. Too many memories and too close to Dave." I rolled my eyes.

"Well, good for you! I always thought you should get a fresh start." She poured some wine into both our glasses. "So how are you feeling? And how's the lover boy?"

I grabbed my wine and took a big chug with hopes the wine would kick in quickly and make this conversation that I didn't want to have, easier. "I'm doing okay, I guess." I took another sip of my wine. "I haven't talked to him."

"What? Why not?"

"I honestly don't know. He woke up and didn't want to see anyone and then his mom took him back to Hawaii, and I don't think anyone has seen or heard from him since. Everyone keeps saying he just needs some time, but I really don't know what to think about it all." I took another chug of my wine. "I mean one minute he's telling me he loves me and wants to marry me, then he jumps in front of a bullet for me and almost dies, and now wants nothing to do with me. Kind of a lot to process."

"Amber, the man jumped in front of a bullet for you. No one does that unless they're madly in love."

"Well, maybe that bullet made him come to his senses. We're just different people from different worlds. I was kidding myself thinking what we had was real." I felt the tears coming but fought them back. "I should have known better."

"Known better? Amber, you have to take these chances, or you'll never find love or happiness. I haven't seen you that happy *ever*." She put extra emphasis on the word ever. "Am I wrong?"

"No, you're right." I rolled my eyes because I hated that she was right. "I was very happy. He showed me happiness and love like I've never known before." I finished off my glass of wine. "Which is why I don't know how to move forward from here. He changed me in a way I can't explain."

I needed to change the subject. "So, what about you? Any new men in your life?"

"No. I went out on a few dates while you were gone, but they were all duds." She poured more wine into my glass. "Is that a tattoo?" She grabbed my wrist.

"Yeah. Didn't I tell you about that? Kris made me get it." I smiled at the memory.

"No, you never told me that! What other little hidden secrets are you hiding from me?"

"Secrets? I'm an open book," I teased.

"Amber, you're the tightest closed book there ever was." She laughed.

"Yeah, yeah." I cracked a smile as the doorbell rang. "Seriously, no one ever comes to visit, and now this is the third person tonight."

"Third? Who else came by?" Julie asked.

"Dave paid me a visit to bitch about me selling the house," I said as I walked to the door.

"Oh, so he is the asshole that almost ran me over when I was walking up. What a douchebag," Julie yelled after me.

I peeked out the window to make sure it wasn't Dave again, and I was shocked to see Shawn standing there. I opened the door. I felt horrible because I knew he had tried to reach me a few times and I hadn't responded.

"So, you are alive?" he jokingly said.

"I know, I'm horrible, and I owe you an apology." I gave him a big hug as he stepped inside. "What are you doing here and how did you know where I lived?"

"You're not hard to find. Have you noticed Kris's security out front?" he said as he pointed to the black SUV.

"Security? Wait, I thought that was paparazzi. He had a camera and was taking pictures." I stared at him questioningly.

"Nope, that's security. I'm just as surprised as you are. Apparently, I'm not the only one worried about you."

"I'm sorry you were worried. I know I'm an asshole for not texting you back. I just… couldn't face anyone. You know?"

"No hard feelings. I didn't mean to just show up, but I was in town visiting my daughter at school for the weekend and thought I would just make sure you were okay."

"Thank you. I'm doing okay, I guess." I hugged him again. "So back to this security thing. Kris won't talk to me, but has people stalking me?"

"He still hasn't reached out?"

"Nope. Nothing."

"I haven't heard from him either." He shook his head. "Typical Kris to have security out here."

"Yeah, typical," I said repeating his statement as I looked out at the SUV across the street. I was confused as to why he would have security watching me. It wasn't like I was in danger and if he cared about me, why didn't he reach out himself?

"Amber, who was at the door?" Julie asked as she turned the corner and stopped dead in her tracks. "Oh, hey there. I'm Julie," she said as she pushed past me to shake Shawn's hand.

"Julie, this is, Shawn. Shawn, this is my best friend, Julie."

"Nice to meet you, Julie." Shawn smiled.

"Shawn, I'm a big fan. I love your music," Julie boasted. "Are you joining us? Come. Sit." She grabbed his hand and dragged him into the living room, not giving him a choice. She looked back at me and raised her eyebrows and smiled. "Amber, get another glass."

Damn, I know what that look means! I grabbed another glass and joined them back in the living room. They were already deep in conversation getting to know each other. Why had I not thought about setting them up before? They were so perfect for each other.

I hung out with them for a little while. It was nice to see both Shawn and Julie laughing; they both deserved to find someone good in their life. I started to feel like a third wheel. I saw how well they were getting along, so I thought it was best that I excused myself.

"You two are welcome to stay and hang out, but I've had a long week, and I'm going to head to bed."

"Amber, hang out with us a little longer," Julie begged.

Shawn stood up. "It's getting late. I should probably head out." He walked over and gave me a hug.

"No, really. You two stay and hang out. I don't mind," I reassured them. "And Shawn, thank you so much for checking on me even after I was a total asshole. I really am sorry."

"You don't have to apologize. I know what you're going through isn't easy."

"Yeah, but you were going through it too, and I'm sorry I wasn't a better friend." I frowned.

Julie chimed in. "Shawn, I know a place we can maybe get some coffee if you're up for it."

"Go. Have fun," I whispered to him.

"You sure you're okay?" he asked.

"Define okay." I laughed. "You two have fun! Julie, call me tomorrow," I said as I made my exit and headed for my room.

I looked out my bedroom window and watched the two of them get in Shawn's car and drive off.

The black SUV was still sitting across the street and had not moved from its original spot. *What are you up to, Mr. August?* I didn't know if I should be mad that he was being creepy and spying on me or take it as a sign of hope that maybe, just maybe he still cared.

I contemplated texting him and asking him why it was necessary. I was wondering if there was another threat that I needed to be worried about. I even typed the message, but then deleted it before I could send it.

I opened my music app instead and hit shuffle. *Don't Fear the Reaper* started playing and it instantly made my heart race. The memory of Kris sitting in that room alone, looking so sad playing that song flooded my head. It tore my heart in two. I could feel the pain he was in then, and it's like I could feel the pain he was in now. *Impossible.*

He's thousands of miles away, and I'm sure he's getting on with life just fine. Unlike me. I just sat there, gazing up at the stars, wondering what Kris was doing at this very moment. Is he thinking about me? Did he miss me? Did his body ache for me like mine ached for him?

———

THE NEXT MORNING, I WOKE TO TEXTS FROM BOTH JULIE AND Shawn. They had definitely hit it off and seemed very excited about the prospect of a possible relationship with each other. That put a smile on my face.

I spent my day putting the final touches on my story since I had promised Rebecca I would have it to her this afternoon. It was scheduled to go out on Monday in a special edition, so I needed to focus and get it done. I felt a bit emotional about finishing it. Part of me was excited to put it behind me, but the other part of me felt devastated. It felt like if I completed this story, it was officially the end of my journey: a journey I wasn't ready to end.

I took a deep breath and hit send. It was done. Come Monday, the world would know what an amazing band The Right Stuff is and what an amazing man Kris August is.

I felt lost. What came next? I did the only thing that felt right: I wrote. The story I told for the magazine was just a small piece, and I had so much more to tell. I had to get it out.

The weekend came and went, and I wrote.

I didn't want to stop writing, so I called in sick to work over the next week and eventually gave my resignation. I thought I enjoyed my job, but I realized, like everything else in my life, I just didn't know any better. I actually hated it. Life was too short to do something I hated, so I quit. I had a nice savings and once I sold the house and downsized I could live off that money for a while until I found something else to do. But until then, I just wrote.

I didn't leave the house often, and when I did, it was because there was a showing at my house or I needed to pick up necessities.

That black SUV still followed me every day and every-where, yet still no word from Kris. After a few weeks, the news even stopped covering the story because there was nothing to cover. It was just like he disappeared. I read online that his show was set to start filming again in a few weeks His people made a statement that he did plan to return to work in time and the show would continue as planned. But that was it. No pictures, no appearances, no other information on his condition. Nothing.

I had to assume that if he was returning to work that meant he was doing well. *I wonder if he saw my story?*

My house sold quickly, and I found a small one-bedroom apartment that I could live in temporarily until I found a place to settle. When I wasn't writing, I spent my days packing and cleaning out the house. Downsizing from a house to an apartment wasn't going to be an easy task.

Today I was tackling my beloved books. I loved books but didn't really have room for them in my apartment.

I was packing them in boxes to donate when I came upon Dante Alighieri's Divine Comedy. *Oh, how I missed my Dante.* I sat down on the floor and just hugged the book. It would forever remind me of Kris, and I couldn't bear to part with it. I carried the book into my bedroom and placed it on my nightstand so I could read it again.

Kris told me once that he thought I saved him, but I think it was the other way around; he saved me, in more ways than one, and I couldn't ever forget that.

I heard my phone ringing. It was a number I didn't recognize, which normally I wouldn't answer, but my heart was still hoping one day it would be Kris, so I answered.

"Hello?" I cautiously answered.

"Is this Amber Johnson?" a man asked.

"Yes. Who's this?"

"I'm Jack Knight. I'm legal counsel for Kris August."

My heart stopped. "Is everything okay?"

"Yes, Ms. Johnson. There is no reason for concern. The reason for my call today is I was hoping to set up a time to meet with you about a settlement offer on behalf of Mr. August and The Right Stuff. It's my understanding that you were injured in the shooting incident involving Mr. August and an employee of The Right Stuff while on tour with the band. Is that correct?"

"Yes, but..." I didn't really know how to respond; I was so confused. "Settlement offer? Mr. Knight, I'm not pursuing a settlement."

"Yes, I'm aware, Ms. Johnson. This is an offer that Mr. August and The Right Stuff are making to compensate you for your injury while on tour. I'll be flying into town tomorrow, and I was hoping I could set up a time to meet with you to go over everything. I believe you will find it to be a very reasonable offer."

What the fuck? "Are you kidding me? Is this a joke?"

"No. I'm sorry, Ms. Johnson. This is not a joke."

"I don't want his fucking money!" I was so angry and hurt that he was sending his lawyer to talk to me instead of facing me. And the fact that he would even think I would want his money sickened me. Knots started to form in my stomach. "Tell Kris..." I paused. I had no idea what to tell Kris. I loved him, I missed him, I needed him, I hated him for doing this to me. No, I couldn't say any of those. "Tell Kris he owes me nothing and I want nothing from him. I'll sign whatever you need me to, but I don't want anything."

"Ms. Johnson, Mr. August was very adamant about ensuring you were compensated for your trouble and––"

I cut him off. "Mr. Knight, nothing he could give me could compensate me for my *trouble*. If that's what he wants to call it. What time tomorrow and where?" I pointedly asked.

"Ms. Johnson, I––"

"Time and place, Mr. Knight! I don't really care what Mr. August wants right now. Feel free to share that with him," I angrily stated.

"Yes, Ms. Johnson. Will tomorrow at noon work for you? I can meet you at the Starbucks on Main Street."

"I'll be there," I said before I abruptly hung up the phone.

The phone almost immediately rang again, and I assumed it was Mr. Knight calling me back. "What now?" I angrily answered.

"Damn, girl! What's got you all pissed off?" Julie said.

"Julie? Shit. I'm so sorry. I thought you were... Never mind. It doesn't matter. What's up?"

"Well, I'm guessing from the mood you're in, this might

not be the best time, but, what would you say to going on a date?"

"Seriously, Julie?"

"Just hear me out. It's someone I met on a dating site, and I'm kind of into Shawn right now, but he's too good to pass up, and I think he would be perfect for you. Please, just one date," she begged. "He's really nice and a fucking hot piece of ass. Just what you need to get your mind off of Kris."

Ugh, that name. I was so angry with him. "You know what? Yeah. I'll go," I blurted out of anger. *Oh God, did I just say that out loud? Fuck!* I really didn't want to do this, but I couldn't exactly sit around waiting forever for some man that obviously didn't want me.

"For real? Yay, Amber! I'm so excited. I promise you won't be disappointed. I'll make all the arrangements. Yay!" she yelled into the phone so loudly I had to pull the phone away from my ear. "Does Friday work?"

"Like in two days? I…"

"Yes, this Friday. I don't want to give you too much time to change your mind. I know how you are, girl!"

I sighed. "Yeah, I guess that will work. Just let me know where."

"Yay!" she squealed again.

"Hey, Julie? Um, do you think maybe you could go shopping with me to help me find something to wear?"

"I thought you would never ask! Of course! How about over lunch tomorrow? Some of us still have jobs you know."

"Funny," I sarcastically said. "That works. Can you meet me at the Starbucks on Main a little past noon?"

"That works! See you tomorrow."

"Thank you, Julie. See you tomorrow." I hung up the phone and the realization of what I just agreed to settled in. That knot in my stomach was now ten times the size, and I wanted to hurl.

The next day I walked into the Starbucks right at noon; I didn't want to spend any more time there than I had to. A gentleman in a suit stood up and waved to get my attention the second I arrived. He was a lot younger than I expected.

"Ms. Johnson?"

"Yes, are you Mr. Knight?"

"Yes. Nice to meet you." He put his hand out for me to shake. "Please sit. I ordered you a coffee, I hope you don't mind." He gestured to the coffee cup on the table.

"Thank you, Mr. Knight. That was very thoughtful, but not necessary." I sat down.

"Ms. Johnson, first I want to start off by saying that--"

I cut him off. "Look, Mr. Knight, please don't take this personally, but I just want to sign this paper and move on with my life. I don't really care what Mr. August wants to offer or wants you to say."

He laughed.

"What's so funny?" I questioned.

"Sorry, it's just that he warned me--"

"Warned you? He needed to warn you about me?" I laughed. "Ha!"

"No, no. I didn't mean it like that. He--"

"Mr. Knight, like I said, I don't want to discuss Mr. August. Please let's just cut the small talk and get this paper signed."

"Of course, Ms. Johnson," he said as he pulled a file out of his bag. "So, by signing--"

"I don't care." I just snatched it from him and signed. I handed it back to him. I saw Julie walk in, right on time, providing me the perfect excuse to leave. "Are we done?"

"Hey, girl! You didn't tell me you were on a date. Look at you go. Two in a row!" She pulled out her chair as if she was going to join us.

"Seriously! It's not a date, and we're leaving so don't sit down," I told Julie. "Are we done, Mr. Knight?"

"Yes, but do you even want to read it?"

"Nope. Don't care." I stood up and decided I would at least take the free coffee. "Thanks for the coffee." I raised the cup and walked away. "Julie, you coming?"

"What was that all about?" she questioned me as we walked out the door.

"It doesn't matter." I took a sip of the coffee, and the all too familiar flavor of peppermint mocha invaded my senses. Of course. My favorite and I imagine Kris had something to do with that. *Fucker!*

I walked passed the black SUV that was tailing me everywhere I went and held up the cup and then made sure he saw me throw it in the trash. As if making a point to Kris that I was done. He can't cut me out of his life without an explanation and then try to still be in it through spying on me and sending other people to meet with me.

"Whoa, what's gotten into you?" Julie asked questioning my out-of-character behavior.

"Just moving on. That's all. Let's go find me something to wear." I forced a smile, but deep inside another piece of me was dying as my heart broke even more.

"I'm so excited! First stop is Victoria's Secret!"

"Great," I sarcastically said as I got into her car.

SHOPPING WITH JULIE WAS ACTUALLY MORE FUN THAN I'D expected. I found some sexy pieces at Victoria's Secret; not like anyone was going to see them, but I felt good in them. I got to hear all about her and Shawn. Apparently, they talked all the time, and he was planning another trip back soon to see her.

"Let's look in here," Julie excitedly said as she pulled me into the next store.

"Forever 21?" I questioned Julie. "Seriously, Julie, for one I'm too old for this shit, and none of this is going to fit me."

"Chill, Amber. It doesn't hurt to look." She grabbed a very tight-fitting dress off the rack. "What about this?"

I laughed. "You're kidding, right? That wouldn't even fit my left ass cheek."

"Whatever, I think it's cute," she said to herself as she put it back on the rack. "Oh, now this one is perfect!" She grabbed another one that I still wasn't crazy about, but at least looked like it might fit.

"Where is he even taking me? Do I need a dress?"

"Fancy restaurant in the city. Yes, you need a dress." She grabbed two more off the rack. "Here. Go try these on."

"Ugh. Do I have to?" I felt like a salty teenager shopping with their mother who was picking out their clothes for them.

"Yes, go!" she demanded.

"Fine!" I stormed into the dressing room, slammed the door shut, and stripped my clothes off.

The first dress was so tight that I couldn't even get it on. "I hate you so bad right now!" I yelled out to Julie that was anxiously waiting on the other side of the door. I threw the dress at her under the door.

"Oh, I liked that one. What's wrong with it?"

"Too fucking tight. Like I said it would be!" I picked up the next dress. "This is so fucking stupid! Can we please go to a store for adults!" I yelled at her.

"What's with all the f-bombs? You're so angry. You know what you need?"

I didn't answer.

"You need to get laid, Amber. This guy tomorrow. He'll fix that. He'll fuck the anger right out of you." She laughed.

I still didn't respond. Mainly because I was too busy trying to figure out how to put the dress on. The straps were so confusing I didn't know if they went in the front or the back and it was of course super tight and I had to do some major dance moves to squeeze into it. I opened the door. "I don't get it. Did I do it wrong? Where does this part go?" I asked as I lifted an extra strap to show her.

Julie started laughing hysterically. "Amber you have it on backward."

"Have I told you how much I hate you right now?"

I looked in the mirror trying to figure out how she could tell. "I don't get it. How can you tell?" I started cracking up. I couldn't even keep a straight face when I saw how stupid I looked in the mirror. It felt good to laugh again. It had been too long.

"Yeah, that's a no. Just go take that one off." She was bent over laughing.

I returned to the dressing room and ripped that one off and squeezed into the third and final dress. It was tight but fit. Definitely not my style. It was red, short and cut way to low in front. I was exposed for the whole world to see. Not really the vibe I wanted to put off on a first date. I stepped out to show Julie.

"Yes! That's it!"

"You're kidding, right? I can't wear this!" I shouted at her.

"Why not. It looks great on you."

"Well for one, there isn't enough of it."

"Stop being a prude. It's sexy!"

"I'm not a prude!" I looked in the mirror again. I would say slutty was a better word to describe the dress. *Am I really a prude?*

Is this what people wear on dates? Fuck if I know! "Really? This is what people wear on dates?" I looked at her hoping she would tell me she was fucking with me, but she didn't. She was dead serious.

"Yes! Get it. Just trust me. And I can come over tomorrow before he picks you up and I can help you with your hair and makeup. He won't be able to keep his hands off you."

"That sounds…great." Not really. That sounded horrible. I faked a smile. I returned to the dressing room and changed back into my clothes and took one last look at the dress on the hanger. *Time to do things a little differently, I guess.*

THE NEXT NIGHT, JULIE CAME OVER AS PROMISED AND HELPED me get ready for my date. She did my hair and my makeup and gave me all sorts of dating tips. None of which I was going to follow, but I nodded and pretended like I was into what she was saying. But I wasn't. I didn't want to do any of this, but I knew I needed to. I felt sick to my stomach and was constantly trying to think of ways to get out of this, but I knew I would never live this down if I backed out.

As I was putting on my hideous dress, the book on my nightstand caught my eye. As angry as I was at Kris, I couldn't stop thinking of him. I missed my Dante horribly, yet here I was about to go out on a date with some dude I didn't even know.

"You waxed right?" Julie snapped me back to reality. "Oh, we should have taken you to that place in the mall, where they can add jewels and decorations to your lady bits."

"Julie, I am not going to vajazzle my vagina! Plus, I don't need all that because I'm already so fabulous that I cum glitter," I teased her, then let out a nervous laugh and quickly changed the subject.

"So, what about this hideous scar on my arm? Is it noticeable?" I asked her as I checked out my arm that is a constant reminder of what happened. It had actually healed nicely, but the scar would be there forever.

"It's fine. You can hardly see it," she reassured me.

Liar!

The doorbell. *Fuck!*

"You ready?" Julie excitedly asked.

"Nope. Nope, not ready." I paced back and forth, before finally getting enough nerve to answer the door. The walk to the front door was the longest walk ever. It felt like an eternity. I took a deep breath, and opened the door.

"Amber?" A tall, decent looking man dressed in a nice suit asked.

"Yes, hi."

"I'm Mark. Wow, Julie said you were hot. You look amazing." He looked me up and down. He couldn't even tear his eyes away from my exposed chest to look me in the eyes. *God, I hate this dress.*

I was ready to get this over with. I grabbed my purse off the table. "Are you ready?" I asked as I stepped out the door, joining him on the front porch.

"Definitely," he enthusiastically said as he walked to this car, a flashy, very expensive Porsche.

I hate Porsches. I preferred American muscle over prestigious foreign cars. *I wonder what he is overcompensating for?* I laughed to myself as he pulled out of the driveway. Of course, that black SUV followed. *Great. This could get interesting.*

The drive to the city was long, thanks to traffic, and it was super awkward. I hated small talk. I never knew what to say. It was so forced and unnatural.

I was so thankful when we pulled up to the restaurant, but then remembered I still had a whole night of awkwardness to get through.

I stepped out of the car and waited for Mark to hand the keys over to the valet, listening as he gave the kid very detailed instructions on how to drive his precious car. *What a douche!*

I was already so over this guy. I was constantly trying to

think of a good excuse to get out of the rest of this date, but the best thing I could think of was telling him I had diarrhea and needed to leave. I needed to keep working on that one.

"Ladies first," he said as he motioned toward the door and placed his hand on the small of my back. His touch creeped me out, but I smiled politely as I entered the restaurant.

We were seated quickly, and he slipped the hostess a big tip. *Yeah, not impressed, buddy.* I couldn't believe Julie thought I would like this guy. I was beginning to think we may not really be friends. I thought for sure she was punking me.

"Would you like some wine?" he asked me.

"Yes!" I enthusiastically answered. *Wine will make this better for sure!*

"So, Julie told me you're a writer?"

"Yes. Well, I'm currently unemployed, but I'm working on a book."

"What kind of book?" he asked as he stared at my tits.

The waiter returned with our wine. *Perfect timing.* I went to grab the glass, but his hand met mine. I gently tried to pull back, but he had a firm grip. *All righty then, I guess he wants to hold hands.*

I rolled my eyes, but I guarantee he didn't see because his eyes hadn't looked up at my face all night. I heard some commotion toward the front of the restaurant and turned to look to see what was going on because I was sure it was more exciting than what was going on at my table.

"Kris!" I yelled as I watched him storm his way through the restaurant. I stood up as he reached the table. "What are you--"

He didn't even give me a chance to finish my sentence. Without a word, he picked me up and threw me over his shoulder.

His touch ignited my body, but his actions infuriated me. My heart was racing and my head was spinning. I was so shocked to see him, I didn't even have time to process what was happening.

"What the fuck, dude. That's my date!" I heard Mark yell as Kris carried me out of the restaurant with everyone watching and recording the whole incident.

"Kris! Stop! What are you doing? Put me the fuck down!" I screamed at him.

He set me down and still didn't say a word. His beautiful dark eyes staring deep into my soul.

There were so many things I wanted to say, but I was at a loss for words. I couldn't decide if I wanted to take him right here in the street or run away. I was so angry and most of all hurt about what he did to me. He left me, and I wasn't sure I could forgive him for that.

"What the fuck, August!" I yelled at him. "Don't you have anything to say?" Still nothing. So, I let it all out. "It's been a month, Kris! A month! And not one word from you. You left me. You left me when I needed you the most." As hard as I tried to fight them back, the tears started to seep out of my eyes.

"Then you have me followed and send people to pay me off? And then you storm in here and carry me out as if you own me!" I paused. "Why, Kris? Don't I at least deserve to know why?" I just looked at him, waiting for answers. His face was full of pain.

"Were you on a date with that guy?" he finally spoke.

"Seriously, August? That's none of your business. But I think you already know the answer to that question. Don't you? I mean your *security* detail wasn't for my safety. It was for you to keep tabs on me. Wasn't it?"

I paused to give him a chance to respond, but he just ran his hand through his hair and looked down at the ground. "Why do you even care, Kris? Why keep tabs on me? Why show up here tonight? It's not like you fucking care about me!

If you cared, you would have let me be there for you. You wouldn't have sent me away and then ignored me for a month!"

He was still looking at the ground. "I'm done!" I turned to walk away.

"I care for you more than I have ever cared about anyone or anything!" he yelled. "Amber, please!"

I stopped and turned around.

He took a few steps toward me, looking me straight in the eyes with a glare of lust mixed with pain. "I love you so much it fucking hurts."

He softly grabbed my hands and pulled me closer to him. "When I walked onto that bus and saw Jen with that gun, I thought I was going to lose you. I would have never been able to live with myself if anything happened to you. That was the worst feeling in the world and then knowing that you were in that situation because of me..." I saw a tear drop down his cheek.

He tenderly touched my arm where I had been shot. "I realized that if I loved you, I needed to let you go in order to keep you safe. It was just better if I wasn't in your life." He gently wiped the tears from my cheek. "Amber, I'm so sorry for putting you in that situation, and I know I didn't handle this right. I was a fucking coward and ran."

His hand trailed down my jaw as he leaned in closer. His other hand wrapped around my waist. "I fucking missed you so much," he whispered in my ear. "I'm weak. I can't stay away from you anymore. I know that's selfish of me, but I need you. I can't live without you." I felt one of his tears drop on my bare shoulder. "Baby, please forgive me. I'm so sorry. Please," he begged.

His touch had my body on fire. He was so close I know he could feel my heart rapidly beating against his chest. My breathing was quick.

"Kris." I pulled away and placed my hands on his cheeks. I hated seeing him like this. I wanted to kiss him. I wanted to take his pain away. I wanted to respond, but I had so many questions and didn't know where to start.

I noticed a crowd was forming around us; this wasn't the place. "Can we go someplace a little more private and talk?"

"I know a place not too far from here." He took my hand, and we walked in silence for a few blocks. We stopped outside the Four Seasons Hotel. "Will this do? I stay here sometimes when filming goes late, and I don't want to drive home."

"Bringing me to a hotel and I'm dressed like a hooker. This night just keeps getting better," I joked.

"Yeah, what's with that dress?" he teased. "Not that I don't enjoy the view, but since when do you dress like that? What happened to comfort and practical, not slutty and whorish?" He laughed as he quoted my exact words from early in the tour.

"I don't really know how to do the whole dating thing, and I let my crazy friend talk me into some really bad choices."

"So, it was a date?" he asked as we walked up to the check-in counter.

"Hello, Mr. August. Usual room?" the perky little blond behind the counter asked.

"Yes, thank you," he responded and turned his attention back to me for a response.

"Yes, it was a date." I rolled my eyes at him and exhaled like I had been holding my breath. "Shit, I just left him there," I said to myself as I realized I had left him without a word.

"Here you go, Mr. August," the desk clerk said as she slid him the room key.

We headed to the elevator.

"Must not have been a good date if you just left him there," he said.

"Well, I was kind of dragged out of there against my will."

He smirked as he pressed the button for the private penthouse elevator and the doors opened. "Do you want to go back?" he asked as he placed his hand on the small of my back and guided me into the elevator. The door shut and he pulled me close to him. "So, do you want to go back?" he slowly and pointedly asked again.

His touch took my breath away. "No," I gasped.

"Good," he said as he grabbed the back of my neck and kissed me with inexplicable hunger. The elevator doors opened, and we stumbled into the expansive and lavish suite without breaking contact, our bodies uncontrollably yearning for each other after a month of deprivation. He quickly removed my dress and carried me to the bedroom.

I pulled off his shirt and froze when I saw the reminder of what happened. A reminder that will be with him forever. He had a pretty large scar that was still healing. It broke my heart. I gently touched it. "Does it still hurt?" I asked as I slowly followed his scar to his back.

"I have good days and bad days," he said.

I kissed where it had torn through his tattoo.

"I went to see James and he's working on a design to cover up the scars once they heal."

I laid down on the bed and pulled him to me. "They wouldn't let me see you, even before you woke up." I rested my head on his chest.

"Then how did you get into my room?" he questioned.

"What? How do you know I was in your room?" I sat up in shock.

"The first thing I remember was hearing you say you loved me. It's kind of fuzzy, but I could hear you and feel you lying next to me." He pulled me back down to his chest and kissed my head. "Just like this. But I couldn't respond or move. It's like you brought me back from wherever I was. You reminded me I have something to live for, to fight for."

"But then you woke up and wanted nothing to do with me."

"Amber, I wanted nothing more than to be with you. I admit I was scared. I was a coward. I thought you would be better off without me, which I still think is true. But when I heard you were going on a date, it fucking killed me. Then when I saw him put his hands on you, I snapped. I don't want to live without you anymore. I've waited for you my whole life, and I don't want to waste another day without you."

He claimed my mouth in a slow passionate kiss while his hand slowly trailed down my stomach and slid under my panties, teasing my swollen and wet opening. There was so much I still wanted to say, but his touch mixed with his intoxicating scent scrambled my brain. He was a drug that I was addicted to. I was still so angry at him, but I was weak; I had no control. I needed him inside me more than I needed anything at the moment.

I unzipped his jeans and freed his raging erection. He slithered my panties off, staring at me with his dark, hungry eyes as he kissed and teased his way up my body. His tongue danced around my sensitive center of pleasure, making me cry out for him, begging for release. A release he wasn't ready to give me.

He continued his way up my body, nibbling my hardened nipples before he returned to my mouth. I could taste my excitement on his lips.

I raised my hips, trying to find him. The engorged tip of his cock slid softly against my throbbing clit, again and again, sending waves of pleasure through my body.

I grabbed the sheets as I cried out, breathlessly demanding him take me. I was so close my body was quivering with need as he finally entered my wet core, stretching me with every thrust.

Our bodies became one. There was no greater feeling than

his throbbing, hard manhood inside me. Mixed with the sounds of his pleasure, I came quickly and harder than I had ever before. I came undone under him as my muscles clenched his shaft, pleading for more. I couldn't breathe, think, or speak.

My nails dug deep into his back as his mouth crashed down on my shoulder. His thrusts becoming harder and faster, finding the sensitive spot deep inside me, causing another intense, deep organism to crash through my body. My liquid desire covered his throbbing cock as he came deep inside me.

We were silent. The only sounds were our haggard breaths that gradually slowed as we fell asleep still entangled in each other's embrace.

The next morning when I woke Kris was still sound asleep, and I didn't want to wake him. I thought it would be nice to grab us some coffee and breakfast. I searched around the room for my clothes, which were strewn all over. God knows I didn't want to put that hideous dress back on, but I didn't really have any other options. I found everything but my damn bra.

I picked up Kris's jeans with hopes that my bra was under them and a little box fell out of his pocket. It was wrapped in the note I gave to his mom at the hospital. It looked like a ring box. *What the fuck?* Was he planning to propose?

I picked up the note and the pain from that moment came rushing back to me. My heart sank into my stomach and that all too familiar knot returned. I quickly stuffed the box and my note back in his pocket.

I looked at Kris lying there sleeping. He looked so happy and peaceful. I loved him, right? Or was it just lust? I was still so confused about him. He still hadn't told me about his "dark past" and that terrified me. Was he hiding something? Could I really marry him?

I barely knew him, yet I felt powerless to say no to him. He was a drug I craved and was terrified of. The power he had over me: to hurt me, to ruin me, triggered panic to run through my body which caused me to do something I knew I would regret forever.

I did the only thing I knew how to do. I took one last look and walked out.

Maybe I was better off alone.

BONUS MATERIAL

NEED A LITTLE MORE? TAKE A LOOK INTO KRIS'S THOUGHTS AND JOURNEY DURING PART 3.

KRIS

I could hear Amber and feel her lying next to me. I couldn't quite make out what she was saying, but I could tell she was upset, and it was destroying me. I wanted to tell her I'm okay. I wanted to hold her, but I couldn't speak or move. Was this a dream? Where was I? Why was I in so much pain? I had no sense of time, and I was completely lost.

Where did she go? I can't feel her anymore. I tried to call out to her, but still, nothing came out. I tried for what seemed like an entirety.

"Amber," I finally heard myself say. "Amber," I said a little louder as I found my voice.

"Kris!" I heard someone yell. "Nurse, I think he's waking up! Kris! I'm here!"

I felt someone grab my hand. "Amber?" I fought to open my eyes.

"Kris, It's Mom! I'm here."

My eyes finally opened. "Mom? Where am I? Where's Amber?" The room was blurry, and I could hear a frenzy of activity around me.

Someone shined a bright light in my eyes, and I swatted them away. *What the fuck?*

"Mr. August, I need to give you an exam. Mr. August, can you understand me?" I heard the woman with the light say.

"What's going on? Where's Amber?" I asked again.

"Mr. August, you're in the hospital. Do you remember what happened to you?" I heard the woman with the light ask.

I tried to think back. Hospital? Why would I be in the hospital?

The memories came rushing back to me like the nightmare that they were. Jen with the gun. Amber in the line of fire.

I remembered that I jumped in front of Amber and tried to get her out of the way. I had to save her. I couldn't live without her. That's the last thing I remembered.

"Oh, God! Is she alive? Is Amber alive? Please, someone, tell me if she's okay." I started to get out of bed. I needed to find her. I was entangled in wires; they were everywhere. I ripped them off. I needed to get up.

"Mr. August, she's fine. I need you to lie back down. You need to rest. Please, Mr. August," the nurse pleaded with me, and she tried to hold me down.

"Kris, Amber is fine. Please lay back down. She's being released from the hospital today. She's fine," my mom said.

"Released from the hospital? What the fuck happened?" I demanded.

"She sustained a minor injury during the incident."

"How did this happen? Did they catch Jen? What the fuck is going on?" I pleaded.

"Well, according to the police, Jen was obsessed with you and wanted to kill Amber out of jealousy. Jen shot you instead of Amber, and then Jen took her own life. Amber is fine, she got shot in the arm. It's a minor injury. She's fine and being released today. I haven't seen her yet, but I was told she's good. Kris, you almost died."

My heart sank. This was my fault, of course. I put her in danger. The woman I had waited for my whole life, the only woman I had ever loved, and I put her in harm's way.

Fuck! I laid back down. The room was spinning and pain radiated through my chest.

"I can go get her if you want," my mom said.

"No. I don't want to see anyone." That was a lie. I wanted to see Amber more than anything. But the realization hit me that I was no good for her. She was safer without me in her life.

I looked at the nurse. "When can I get out of here?"

"I'll have the doctor come in, and he'll be able to talk to you about your options," the nurse said as she walked out.

My mom sat down in the chair next to my bed. "Kris, I've made arrangements to bring you back to Hawaii as soon as possible. I think it's best if you come home to recover. You need to get away from all this."

"Fine. Sooner the better." I was too pissed to deal with anyone. I just wanted to leave this hellhole of a hospital, and I didn't really care where I went. I just needed to move on with my life and try to forget about Amber. It was for her own good.

It was late, and I should have been sleeping, but I couldn't. Rage ran through my veins as the details of that night played over and over again in my mind. The look of fear on Amber's face and the look of hate on Jen's face. My heart raced with anger every minute I sat here helpless...and alone.

Memories of Amber kept flooding my mind. The first time I met her when she ran into me and spilled her peppermint mocha all over me. She was so beautiful. And her touch, as brief as it was fucking drove me insane with desire for her.

I could still picture her sitting at that table alone on the first day, listening to Vanilla Ice, not having a care in the world. And how adorable she was when I made her all flustered by just being near her. How red she turned when our eyes met when I was performing on stage. Or how sexy her ass looked in those sweatpants the first night and her sassy fucking attitude.

God, she drove me insane, and I knew I had to have her from that very first moment I met her, and now I have to give her up.

"Kris, are you awake?" I heard my mom whisper as she entered my room.

"Yeah," I grumbled.

"I just went to grab some coffee and Amber is still here. She's such a sweet girl, and she really wants to see you."

She sat down and sighed, "But, I did finally convince her she needed to go to the hotel and get some rest. I really like her Kris, and she seemed crushed. I just don't understand why you don't want to see her. What happened?"

"It's complicated. I really don't want to talk about it."

"I don't think it's that complicated, son. You obviously love her. Why are you pushing her away?"

I couldn't answer her. I just rolled over, wishing I could leave this fucking place already. Tomorrow couldn't get here fast enough.

"Well, she gave this to me to give to you. I'll just leave it here on the table for you."

I turned around and watched as she placed a small piece of paper on the table. I wanted to know what it said, but I wasn't strong enough to look. I knew whatever it said would wreck me, so I refused to look. I closed my eyes and pretended to sleep so I wouldn't have to talk about it anymore.

Early the next morning, I woke and prepared to leave. I still couldn't bring myself to read the note from Amber so I placed it in my pocket where it would stay until I was ready. I was discharged from the hospital and was on my plane headed to Hawaii. The damn press was ruthless and swarmed, but I had nothing to say, not to them or anyone. Even when we arrived on the island, they were everywhere. They were even camped out in front of Mom's house. I told my publicist to provide statements, but I wasn't interested in speaking to anyone about the incident. I didn't plan to leave the house so I hoped they would eventually get tired of waiting and leave. It took a few days, but they did start to thin out once they realized there wasn't a story here.

Every day was the same. It would start with a doctor checking on me at the house followed by a workout with a physical therapist to get the strength back in my arm. I struggled to play my guitar, and I spent hours a day practicing. It was all I could do to keep my mind off Amber, but even that didn't work. Even the music I played made me think of her.

I would never forget the time she was spying on me as I played. Truth be told, she devastated me the night before when she ran out of the party after we danced. She was so different from the other women, and I've never had one run out on me like that. I didn't know how to handle it. But then when I saw her the next morning standing in the door, watching me, her smile told me she was mine, and she looked so fucking hot. I didn't think she was aware that I knew she was there, but I did, and I loved watching her squirm.

Every day I got stronger, physically, but emotionally I got weaker. I just needed to know if she was okay, so I sent some of my security staff to keep watch over her. But the reports I got just made me worry more.

First, she put her house up for sale and then she stopped going to work. *Fuck!*

I couldn't stand being away from her, and I wondered if she felt the same.

Time to check in. I called Charlie, the security detail I put out to watch Amber.

"Charlie, any updates?"

"Hello, Mr. August. I'm outside Ms. Johnson's place, and there's been a lot of activity today. First, a man came to the door. I looked him up, and it's her ex-husband. It was an unfavorable exchange, and she turned him away quickly. Her friend Julie stopped by, followed by Shawn about an hour ago."

"Shawn? What the fuck is he doing there?"

"I'm not sure, Mr. August." He paused. "Shawn and Julie appear to be leaving together. Would you like me to follow them?"

"No, thank you, Charlie. Please stay with Amber. Alert me if there are any more visitors or odd activity."

"Yes, Sir."

I hung up the phone and just stared at it. I wanted so badly to speak to her, to hear her voice again, to feel her in my arms. I opened the last text message I had from her, something I did often.

I wanted to type but was frozen in fear. I was bad for her; I put her in danger, and I needed to stay away.

Shit! The bubble appeared, and it looked like she was typing me a message. I waited, but nothing ever came through. I threw my phone and picked up my guitar. Music was the only thing that helped the pain. Not the pain from the bullet, but the pain from not having her in my life.

I played *Don't Fear the Reaper*, the song that reminded me of her. I didn't know why... Maybe because I was the reaper?

I was bad for her, and as much as I didn't want her to fear me, as much as I wanted to be with her, I feared that by being in her life, her life would end in tragedy, and I couldn't live with myself if anything ever happened to her. Just another fucking tragic love story.

Lost, I sang as I gazed up at the stars. What she was thinking about? What she was doing at that exact moment? Did she still love me? Did her body ache for me like mine ached for her?

I had never craved someone's touch as much as I craved hers. She was a drug, and I was going through withdrawal. I felt like I was going to die without her.

I spent the next few days in bed. I turned away the doctors and skipped physical therapy. I didn't even play my guitar.

My phone had been going off like crazy, and I had been ignoring it.

"Kris!" I heard my mom yell from outside my room. I didn't respond. "Kris, you have a phone call! They said it's important," she said as she barreled into my room. "Get up. Enough of this. Pull yourself together," she said as she pulled the blankets off me and handed me the phone.

"Tell them I'm busy," I told her.

"Kris! Take the phone!" she yelled as she threw it on the bed next to me.

"Fine!" I yelled at her as she ripped the curtains open, exposing me to the blinding sunlight which I hadn't seen in days.

"Hello?"

"And take a shower!" she yelled as she exited my room.

"Kris, it's Jackie."

Great. My publicist. Just who I didn't want to talk to. "Hey, Jackie, this really isn't a good time."

"I know, Kris, but Amber's story was just released, and I thought you would want to know. I emailed you the link. Hope you're well, my friend, the world misses you. My phone rings constantly. People are worried about you."

Her story! I can't believe I forgot about that! I hung up the phone without even responding to Jackie and grabbed my laptop. My heart was racing. I couldn't wait to read what she wrote. I navigated to my email and found Jackie's message with a link to Amber's article and lost myself in her words.

She wrote an amazing story. But it wasn't about me, and it wasn't about us. It was about the band and the fans. Her words were kind, and her story was uplifting. She got it; she got what we were trying to do.

Once again memories of our time together on tour flooded my mind as she referenced them in her story. At the end, she added an out of place quote from Dante's Divine Comedy, *"Lost are we, and are only so far punished. That without hope we live on in desire."*

This may have been out of place for the average reader, but it was a message to me. It's my tattoo. That was us. She was speaking to me. She brought me into the light and yet I found myself back in darkness.

I was so overwhelmed with emotion that I felt tears threatening to fall. I fought them back but lost that battle when I saw the photo of us she included after the quote.

I slammed the laptop shut and stormed into the bathroom. I needed to get out of here. I was lost, and I needed to find myself again. I turned on the shower and ripped off my clothes. I caught a glimpse of my back in the mirror, and I could see where the bullet had torn through my tattoo, the very one Amber quoted in her story. I reminded myself I needed to find my strength and live in the darkness so she could live in the light.

I left a few days later in the middle of the night and flew to Austin, Texas. James was the friend that I always knew I could count on when I needed to be set straight. I arrived around lunchtime, and he met me at the door and welcomed me with open arms.

"Kris! Brotha! Nice to see you! You've been like a ghost lately. No one has seen or heard from you in weeks."

"I know, I know. Been trying to put myself back together again."

"Well, come in. You hungry?" He motioned to the table which had bags of food from my favorite barbeque place.

"Dude! This is amazing. Thank you," I said as I followed him over to the table. I hadn't had much of an appetite lately, but I couldn't pass this up.

"So, I saw the news about you being shot. What happened? How's Amber? I'm surprised she isn't with you."

My head dropped. "Where do I begin?" I shook my head. "James, she was the one. She was the one I was waiting for. Things were going so well, but then Jen, our new road manager, tried to kill her."

"She tried to kill Amber? That's messed up. Why?"

"The police told me Jen was obsessed with me and had been plotting a way to be with me. Then, when I got with Amber, she lost her shit and tried to kill her."

"I saw in the news that she was taken to the hospital as well, but they didn't release any details. Is she okay?"

"I arrived right as Jen was getting ready to shoot her. I knocked Amber down and took the bullet, but it passed through me and got her in the arm." I took a deep breath as I relived that moment, one that haunted my dreams every night.

"That's fucked up."

"I know. But she's fine. She's back home in Chicago." I picked at the food in front of me, no longer hungry.

"And that's why you've been a ghost, isn't it?"

"Ah, you know me so well, James." I let out a fake laugh.

Hoping to change the subject, I took off my shirt. "Hey, do you think you can fix this?" I asked as I showed James where the bullet ripped through my tattoo.

"Damn, Kris. You're lucky to be alive! I had no idea it was that serious." He got up and walked over to take a closer look. "Yeah, I can fix that. It needs to heal for a few months, but I'll take care of it. No worries. You want the same thing or something different?"

"Same thing."

"Kris, you've been in limbo for too long. It's time to move on. What if we did something different? Maybe something for Amber?"

"Amber is no longer in my life," I blurted out. It hurt to say it too.

"Why not?"

"Because I'm fucked up. I'm cursed. I belong in limbo. She's too good for me. If I stayed with her, she would constantly be in danger. I couldn't protect her. It's just better this way."

"That's the stupidest shit I've ever heard! You're fucking kidding me, right?"

"No, I'm serious. It's my fault she got shot. It's because of me. She could have died all because some fucked up employee slash psycho fan was obsessed with me. And to top it off, I hired Jen! I brought that psycho into our lives. And to make it worse, my ex, Lily was stalking us. If they hadn't found her, God knows what would've happened. If Amber's with me, there will always be someone after her. I'm better off alone, James. I need the tattoo back, it's just who I am."

"Kris, that is some narcissistic shit if I've ever heard any. I know you're famous and have had lots of women and they're always throwing themselves at you and all, but really, dude? That doesn't mean someone is always going to be after Amber. That doesn't mean you can't settle down and find love, which, I might add, is something you've always wanted and the reason I gave you that tattoo in the first place. You wanted to find someone to bring you into the light, and you found her. Her name is Amber, and you're the stupidest man alive if you let her get away. Why are you going to let others keep you from living your life the way you want to live it? That is not the Kris August I know. And you jumped in front of a bullet for her. If that isn't crazy love, then I don't know what is."

"Fuck! I messed up, didn't I? I'm such an asshole!" I ran my hand through my hair. "And I'm pretty sure she wouldn't even want anything to do with me at this point. I haven't talked to her since this all went down."

"Happens to the best of us, brother! Love makes us do stupid things. You're welcome to stay as long as you need, but I think you need to head back to Chicago and work this shit out."

"Yeah, you're right. You're always right." I sighed. "I need a little time to get my head straight first. I need to figure out what I need to do to get her back."

I noticed he had his Bible out on the table amongst all the food. "I see you came prepared for me," I said as I pointed at the Bible. "You going to start preaching to me again?"

"Hey, I'll do whatever it takes to get you back on the right path."

My phone rang, which was great timing. I loved James, but I hated when he went all preacher on me. Mostly because he always made me realize shit about myself I didn't want to deal with.

"Charlie! What do you have for me? Everything okay with Amber?"

"Mr. August. Yes, Ms. Johnson is fine, but I thought you'd want to know it appears Ms. Johnson has quit her job and sold her house."

"Fuck!" Panic consumed me because something wasn't right. *What is going on with her?* "Thank you, Charlie. Anything else I need to be aware of?"

"Not at this time, Mr. August. I'll alert you if anything changes."

"Thank you," I said as I hung up and immediately dialed my lawyer.

"Jack, it's Kris. Hey, I need you to do me a favor."

"Kris! How's the healing coming along?" he asked.

"I'm fine. Thanks. Look, I need you to contact Amber Johnson, the woman that was injured on tour with me and offer her money for her injury. Can you make that happen?"

"Is she suing you?"

"No, I just want to find a way to get her money. I'm worried about her and want to make sure she's taken care of. Just make something up if you have to. Can you do that?"

"I'll see what I can do. I can draw up a settlement agreement, maybe. I'll look into it. How much are you wanting to offer?"

"I don't care. Whatever's normal, plus some. Make it generous."

"Okay, I'll see what I can do."

"I want this done tomorrow. Do you think you can meet with her and get this taken care of?

"I'll get my staff on it right away."

"Perfect. Oh, and fair warning, she's going to give you a hard time, and she won't want to take it. Please do what you can to make this appear to be a real thing so she'll take the money. Can you do that?"

"I'll do my best."

"Thank you. Keep me updated."

I hung up the phone to see James giving me his usual I shouldn't have done that look. "What? She obviously needs money, so I'm going to make sure she's taken care of."

"Dude, you don't get it, do you?" he said, and he grabbed his Bible.

Fuck! He was right... I didn't get it. I was a fucking mess. I slid my hands in my pockets and leaned back, preparing myself for some heavy, much-needed conversation. I felt the wrinkled paper in my pocket; the note from Amber. I still hadn't read it, but it was time. I pulled it out and slowly opened it.

I'm sorry. I love you. -A

Those words tore through my heart like a dull blade. *Sorry? What was she sorry for?* Does she blame herself? This was all my fault, and she was apologizing to *me*.

My heart broke more than it already was. I'd hurt her, and she still loved me. At least she did when she wrote this.

I was such a selfish ass. I didn't deserve her, but I couldn't live without her, and I needed to get her back. Forever.

"James, I need your help!" I interrupted him. "I need a ring. Now!"

The next morning, I woke early, ring in my pocket and a new outlook on life. I loved Amber, and I needed her more than I needed anything else. I was a man on a mission. The plane was ready, and I was eager to get back to Chicago...and to Amber.

Jack had texted me to let me know that Amber wouldn't

take the money, which wasn't surprising. She's so unbelievably stubborn, but that's one of the things I love about her. She's independent and doesn't take shit from anyone, especially not from me.

For weeks I'd been having flashbacks of our time together. I could still taste her on my lips, hear her moaning my name, and feel her wet pussy around my cock.

I loved the way her body responded to my touch. I'd never wanted—no needed, a woman as badly as I needed Amber. I had the worst fucking case of blue balls I'd ever had. I thought about her constantly; she had hijacked my thoughts, my soul, and my cock. No woman had ever had this effect on me, ever! I couldn't get back to her fast enough.

When I arrived in Chicago, I touched base with Charlie. I was anxious to learn where she was so I could figure out how I was going to do this. Was I just going to show up? Was I going to randomly run into her? *Ugh, I fucked up!* I needed to find a way to fix it, but how?

Charlie told me she was at her house and her friend Julie was there with her. I needed to catch her alone. I told him to keep me updated. I needed to find the best time; if there ever was one.

I thought it would feel good to be home, but it didn't. It felt empty. I had always lived alone, but for some reason, my life, my house, my heart, suddenly felt void. It was all meaningless without someone to share it with. Without Amber.

How could I have been so stupid? How did I manage to fuck up the best thing in my life? Yeah, I had a great career, nice things, money, but none of that meant anything without her.

I paced as I waited for an update from Charlie. My head was spinning, and I couldn't concentrate on anything.

A few hours later, my phone finally buzzed.

Charlie: *A man arrived, and Amber left with him.*

Me: *Who is this man? Is this a friend or a date?*

Charlie: *They're dressed up. I'm guessing a date, but not sure.*

Me: *Where are they headed? I'm leaving now.*

Charlie: *Looks like they're headed to the city. I'll send you my location so you can follow.*

Fuck! She's on a fucking date?! Panic and jealousy ran through my veins. There was no more time to waste; the time was now. I needed to reclaim the love of my life.

I grabbed the keys to my Challenger, which I knew would get me there quickly, and headed out. I followed the blinking dot on my phone, knowing Charlie was closely behind Amber.

Traffic was horrible, and I was quickly losing my patience as I weaved in and out of cars trying to catch up to where they were.

The blinking dot stopped and not too far away from where I was. Fear almost incapacitated me as I pulled up. I didn't know what I was going to see or if I was going to be able to get her back, but I had to fight. I quickly stopped the car and jumped out.

"Hey buddy, you can't leave your car there," I heard the valet yell at me, but I didn't care. I tossed the keys at him and froze in my tracks when I saw her.

She was wearing a dress that showed way too much and was not her at all, but she still looked beautiful. My heart stopped at the sight of her. Then I saw the douchebag she was with, and anger boiled in me. They walked into the restaurant, and I watched as he placed his hand on the small of her back. It felt like someone punched me in the gut.

This was definitely a date. Had she moved on? I stood there in shock. I didn't know what to do. *Do I walk away or do I go in there and...and...fuck!*

I paced back and forth in front of the door as I tried to figure out what I needed to do. I didn't want to make a scene, but I had to do something. I stepped inside and tried to find where they were seated.

"Sir, can I help you," the hostess asked. But again, I couldn't respond. I had Amber in my sight.

I watched as she looked at the menu and that douchebag stared at her tits and then reached for her hand. I didn't even feel myself walking, but I could hear the hostess yelling at me. "Sir! Sir! You can't go back there!"

But I kept going, and before I knew it, I was at her table. Without a word, I picked her up, threw her over my shoulder and walked out. *Fuck that dude!*

Her body felt amazing pressed up against mine, and her scent was intoxicating. God, I missed her.

I gently set her down on the sidewalk once we were out of the restaurant. I couldn't take my eyes off of her.

"What the fuck, August?" she yelled at me. "Don't you have anything to say?" She paused. "It's been a month, Kris! A month! And not one word from you. You left me. You left me when I needed you the most."

I could see the pain in her eyes as tears fell. It was killing me to see how much I had hurt her.

"Then you have me followed and send people to pay me off? And then you storm in here and carry me out as if you own me!" She paused. "Why, Kris? Don't I at least deserve to know why?" She looked at me, waiting for answers.

Speak, Kris! Say something! "Were you on a date with that guy?" I asked.

"Seriously, August? That's none of your business. But I think you already know the answer to that question. Don't you? I mean your *security* detail wasn't for my safety. It was for you to keep tabs on me, wasn't it?"

I didn't know how to respond. She was right, and I felt like an ass. I ran my hand through my hair and looked down at the ground. I was ashamed, and she had every right to be angry with me. *God, will she ever forgive me?*

"Why do you even care, Kris? Why keep tabs on me? Why show up here tonight? It's not like you fucking care about me! If you cared, you would have let me be there for you. You wouldn't have sent me away and then ignored me for a month! I'm done!" she turned and started to walk away.

Don't let her go, you ass! "I care for you more than I've ever cared about anyone or anything," I yelled. "Amber, please!"

She stopped and turned around.

I took a few steps toward her, looking her straight in those beautiful eyes. I wanted nothing more than to take her right there. "I love you so much it fucking hurts." I softly grabbed her hands and pulled her closer to me. The distance between us was killing me. I needed to feel her.

"When I walked on to that bus and saw Jen with that gun, I thought I was going to lose you. I would have never been able to live with myself if anything happened to you. That was the worst feeling in the world and then knowing that you were in that situation because of me..."

Emotions overwhelmed me as I thought about that night. I felt my eyes fill up with tears and despite my best efforts to fight them back, one escaped and rolled down my cheek. I tenderly touched her arm where she'd been shot. It wrecked me to see that scar, knowing it was there because of me.

"I realized that if I loved you, I needed to let you go to keep you safe. It was just better if I wasn't in your life." I gently wiped the tears from her cheek. "Amber, I'm so sorry for putting you in that situation, and I know I didn't handle this right. I was a fucking coward and ran."

My hand trailed down her jaw, and I leaned in closer and wrapped my other arm around her waist. I couldn't get close enough to her. "God, I fucking missed you so much," I whispered in her ear. "I'm weak. I can't stay away from you anymore. I know that's selfish of me, but I need you. I can't live without you." I felt another tear escape my eyes. "Baby, please forgive me. I'm so sorry. Please," I begged.

"Kris." She pulled away and placed her hands on my cheeks. "Can we go someplace a little more private and talk?"

I did notice a crowd start to form around us. I agreed we needed to get out of here. "I know a place not too far." I took her hand, and we walked in silence for a few blocks. The sheer touch of her hand in mine affected me in a way I couldn't explain. I felt...whole.

We stopped outside the Four Seasons Hotel. "Will this do?" I asked. "I stay here sometimes when filming goes late, and I don't want to drive home."

"Bringing me to a hotel and I'm dressed like a hooker. This night just keeps getting better," she joked.

"Yeah, what's with that dress?" I teased. "Not that I don't enjoy the view, but since when do you dress like that? What happened to comfort and practical, not slutty and whorish?" I laughed as I remembered her slinging that shit at me on one of the first days after she joined us on tour.

"I don't really know how to do the whole dating thing and I let my crazy friend talk me into some really bad choices."

"So, it was a date?" I asked as we walked up to the check-in counter.

"Hello, Mr. August. Usual room?" Emily, the front desk clerk asked.

"Yes, thank you," I said and returned my attention back to Amber, anxious for her answer.

"Yes, it was a date." She rolled her eyes at me and exhaled like she had been holding her breath. She's so fucking adorable. "Shit, I just left him there," I heard her say to herself as if she just realized she had ditched her date. I couldn't hide my smile.

"Here you go, Mr. August," Emily said.

We headed to the elevator.

"Must not have been a good date if you just left him there," I said still grinning from ear to ear.

"Well, I was kind of dragged out of there against my will."

I pressed the button for the private penthouse elevator, and the doors opened. "Do you want to go back?" I asked as I placed my hand on the small of her back and guided her into the elevator. The heat between us was undeniable. The door shut and I pulled her as close to me as I could get her. "So, do you want to go back?" I slowly and pointedly asked again.

"No," she gasped.

"Good," I said as I grabbed the back of her neck and kissed her with a hunger and desire that had lain dormant for forty-three years, awakened only by Amber.

The elevator doors opened, and we stumbled into the suite without breaking contact; our bodies uncontrollably yearning for each other after a month of deprivation. I needed to feel her naked body up against me.

I quickly removed that hideous dress and carried her to the bedroom. She pulled off my shirt and froze. She gently touched my scar, "Does it still hurt?" she asked as she slowly followed the scar around to my back.

"I have good days and bad days," I said, completely lost in her touch.

She kissed where it had torn through my tattoo as if she knew how much it pained me. Her lips were so warm and soft; my heart raced.

"I went to see James and he's working on a design to cover up the scars once they heal."

She laid down on the bed and pulled me to her. "They wouldn't let me see you, even before you woke up," she said as she rested my head on my chest.

"Then how did you get into my room?" I questioned because I knew she had visited me.

"What? How do you know I was in your room?" She sat up.

"The first thing I remember was hearing you say you loved me. It's kind of fuzzy, but I could hear you and feel you lying next to me." I pulled her back down to my chest and kissed her head. It felt so right having her on me. "Just like this, but I couldn't respond or move. It's like you brought me back from wherever I was. You reminded me I have something to live for, to fight for."

"But then you woke up and wanted nothing to do with me."

"Amber, I wanted nothing more than to be with you. I admit I was scared. I was a coward. I thought you'd be better off without me, which I still think is true. But when I heard you were going on a date, it fucking killed me. Then when I saw him put his hand on you, I snapped. I don't want to live without you anymore. I've waited for you my whole life, and I don't want to waste another day without you."

I claimed her mouth, taking my time because I never wanted this to end. My hand slowly trailed down her stomach and slid under her fucking sexy panties, which I then remembered she was wearing for a date with another man. I wanted to tear them off in anger, but then my fingers found her swollen and wet opening and I couldn't think of anything other than being buried deep inside her. She was a drug that I was addicted to. She made me weak; I had no control. I needed to be inside her more than I needed anything at the moment.

She unzipped my jeans and freed my raging erection, and I slithered her panties off, staring into her beautiful eyes.

I kissed and teased my way up her body. *She tasted so fucking good.* Her moans and cries for me only made me tease her more. Those were my favorite sounds in the world, and I couldn't get enough of her. I continued my way up her body, nibbling her hardened nipples. Her tits were the most beautiful I had ever seen. Her curves drove me insane.

I kissed her and I could feel her hips meet mine. She needed me as badly as I needed her. I slid my cock softy against her throbbing clit, again and again. She grabbed the sheets and begged for me to take her. I could feel her body quivering with need beneath me. She was so sexy, I couldn't hold back anymore, I needed to be inside her.

I pushed myself slowly into her slick entrance, just a little at a time; I wanted to savor this feeling. She was so tight and wet for me that our bodies became one. There was no greater feeling than being deep inside her, especially when she came, and her pussy clenched my cock as if begging for more.

I could feel her nails dig deep into my back as I felt her cum again, this time I was powerless over her powers as I came hard, losing myself as only she could make me do.

We were silent. The only sounds were our haggard breaths that gradually slowed as we feel asleep still entangled in each other's embrace.

Tomorrow was a new day; a brighter day and I couldn't wait to start my forever with Amber.

"BE STILL MY HEART" IS THE FIRST BOOK
IN THE "BE STILL" SERIES

CHECK OUT BOOK TWO, "BE STILL MY LOVE"
NOW AVAILABLE ON Amazon.

ABOUT THE AUTHOR

J.L. Feaman is a married, mother of two teenage boys that is a native of the Chicagoland area, but has lived the majority of her adult life in Central Illinois. She works by day in corporate America, but by night she follows her dreams of working as a writer and movie producer.

"I'm not as I appear. I work a corporate job, I'm a wife, and I'm a nice suburban mom, but I'm more than that. I like tattoos, rap music, rock 'n roll; I have a dark side and a creative side that I don't show many people. So, I'm guessing many people will be surprised by the things I write. I used to be afraid to show people the real me. Why? I don't know, but I turned 40 and something clicked. I don't give a fuck anymore! I hope my work will someday inspire others just like me to follow their dreams too! You never know what you are capable of doing until you try.

I hope you enjoy my writing. This is just the beginning."

FOR MORE INFORMATION:
https://jlfeaman.com

 facebook.com/JLFeaman
 twitter.com/JLFeaman

ACKNOWLEDGMENTS

Special thank you to my family for allowing me the time to
follow my dream!

PLAYLIST

Music is a huge part of my life and an inspiration in my writing. I just had to share my playlist for this book. Enjoy!

https://jlfeaman.com/playlists/

Printed in Great Britain
by Amazon